PIECES OF THE GAME

Roger Davenport

Oxford University Press
Oxford New York Toronto

Oxford University Press, Walton Street, Oxford OX2 6DP

Oxford New York Toronto
Delhi Bombay Calcutta Madras Karachi
Kuala Lumpur Singapore Hong Kong Tokyo
Nairobi Dar es Salaam Cape Town
Melbourne Auckland Madrid

and associated companies in
Berlin Ibadan

Oxford is a trade mark of Oxford University Press

Copyright © Roger Davenport 1993
First published 1993

ISBN 0 19 271697 2

A CIP catalogue record for this book is available from
the British Library

Printed and bound in Great Britain
on acid-free paper-
by Biddles Ltd,
Guildford and King's Lynn

TO HARRY

'But helpless Pieces of the Game He plays
Upon this Chequer-board of Nights and Days...'

The Rubaiyat of Omar Khayyam

trans. Edward Fitzgerald

CHAPTER 1

'WILL CHRISTOPHER Lucas please come to the Lost Children's Post, where his parents are waiting for him.'

The woman's voice sounded undisturbed, coming through the loudspeaker system. 'Christopher is eight years old and has fair hair. He is wearing a pale blue anorak and blue jeans.'

In the free-range cage opposite Penny and Nick, a gorilla placed his long arms on the ground and stuck out his bottom. Penny had a fantasy that the great dark creature was making a statement: 'I'm not moving until that child is found. I'm serious.' He looked serious.

'That's Christopher Lucas, who is out in the zoo. Can he re-join his parents at the Lost Children's Post.'

The Tannoy system clicked off. No one had taken any notice of it, although it was by no means cold for November and London Zoo was busy. The warm weight of the overcast sky meant that those visitors who were seasonally dressed, by some strict calendar code, would be sweating into their woollens and body-warmers. Penny had managed to stuff her school raincoat into her shoulder-bag, but Nick carried his smart Puffa jacket with pride. It was so colourful and so absurdly inflated that to Penny's half-envious eye it looked as if he was carrying a rolled-up parachute.

Nick pulled a face at the ape behind the bars. 'That gorilla doesn't half smell.'

Penny stepped back as the heavy acid aroma came to her, too. 'Not his fault.' The gorilla slowly turned his head away from them, though with no discernible emotion. 'You'd smell as well if you didn't wash.'

1

'The other animals don't smell—not many of them,' said Nick, with truth. 'Except in the Children's Zoo.'

'Do you want to go there today?' Penny asked.

'No. Kid's stuff. The whole place is kid's stuff, if you ask me. I don't know why we come here.' The swagger left his voice. 'Actually, have you seen Mum and Dad recently?'

'No. Perhaps they're at the Lost Parents' Post.'

He nearly laughed at that. 'Yeah. Nice one. Come on, let's go to the gift shop.'

As they neared the shop and the playground beside it, a child wearing a very grubby T-shirt inserted himself between them, with difficulty fitting his stride to theirs.

'Got ten pence?'

'No,' said Nick definitely.

'You're going to the shop, though,' the boy accused.

'Go and play with a camel or something. This is a zoo. You're here to look at animals.'

His lofty attitude did not prevent Nick himself from being caught by the attractions of the shop. Bearing in mind her mother's dictum that, 'you don't have to spend money just because you've got it', Penny was amused at how her brother dithered over his choice of purchase, only to leave the shop at last with a leather bookmark he didn't want. Sometimes it was hard to believe that he was more than a year older than she was.

Outside, children chased and scattered pigeons, frustrated by the untouchability of so many of the exhibits. The grubby T-shirt shot by, besotted with the urge to kick at least one living creature if the treasures of the gift shop were to be denied him.

Once out of the shop, Nick was anxious again.

'Where are they, then?'

'Well, they do always say, when in doubt try the elephants' grass.'

'Oh yeah. We could try there, I suppose. In a minute...'
Having established the probable whereabouts of the lost

parents, he was once more in no hurry to join up with them.

The sign on the grass at the perimeter of the zoo read, 'This grass is left uncut for the elephants to eat.' Barbara Hodge was sitting on her coat: the length of the grass had convinced her it must be damp.

Graham Hodge stood beside her, fidgeting a little, with his hands in the pockets of his soft leather jacket. They had not spoken for some moments now and today it had been his jacket which had struck the first sparks of mutual irritation. Barbara had expressed the opinion that to wear a jacket made out of an animal displayed insensitivity when visiting a zoo.

'Insensitivity? To what?' Graham had asked. 'To our dumb chums?'

'Yes — exactly that.'

'They're used to the odd scraps of animal matter. They eat each other,' he had answered. 'I don't think they'll mind one bit, me wearing something made out of a cow.'

'A calf.'

'Yes — all right. A calf. A dear little calf. With a name? Of course. And a nice nature, too — yes? Almost human. Poor little thing.'

He had been pleased with this performance and had spoken into the collar of the jacket, repeating, 'Poor little thing.'

Later they had argued about money in a routine fashion, getting that subject out of the way like an uninteresting soup before the main course. Now they had begun the chief argument of the day, as yet with no outcome.

'Here they come,' said Graham, breaking the silence.

Barbara had already seen her children approaching and had made a mental note to smarten Penny up. She looked dreadfully drab beside her brother. 'Nick looks well,' she said in a neutral tone.

'Why wouldn't he?'

3

'But they don't look very comfortable together today.'

'Well...that's boys and girls for you. At their age — ages.'

'They should see more of each other.'

That old story again, thought Graham. The kids were fine — just fine. Fine, untroubled, healthy young animals. One couldn't expect them to act like twins. They had always had very distinct, different natures. Just as they were physically different. Penny with her calm and stillness, with that open face and dark brown eyes; and Nick with his more bony features and sharp mind: quicker, and taller...Only their identical mousy hair showed their common parentage. Nick's eyes were light green, like Graham's.

On her part, Barbara noticed how much taller Nick was than his sister. He must have shot up over recent months. Soon he would be taller than Graham. Which wasn't saying much... Yet Nick did not have his father's continuous burn of inner energy — that energy that Barbara had, through Graham, come to associate with short men.

Graham muttered, 'Come on, Babs. Look happy.'

Nick was saying, 'They look grim. We'll be cheerful. OK?'

'I'm not going to fake anything,' Penny said. 'That'd just be silly.'

'Just be cheerful,' he repeated firmly. 'That'll make their day.'

'Don't see why it should. They might have more important things to do than think about us. In case that hadn't occurred to you. What with the Toy Boy and all.'

The reference to their recently shared joke made her smile. Nick saved his own grin for when they got closer. He wanted there to be no doubt in his parents' minds that his good spirits were assumed on their behalf. His dad would notice it anyway, though Nick was not sure about his mother. Really, he hardly knew her these days. Had she always looked so serious? Just for a second he recalled from his early childhood the friendly smell of a scent she

4

had worn. Beside her, Dad was very much the little rooster; neat and bright and energetic.

Penny was thinking about the Toy Boy and the smile had left her face. Had she been asked to summarize what she thought about her mother and father she might have said, 'I love my mother for a hundred reasons, although we argue, and I love my father too, but I can't remember why.'

Graham and Barbara were divorced. For the last five years Penny had lived with her mother in London, while Graham and Nick lived in the country, in Cambridgeshire.

'Hi, kids,' Graham called.

Nick called back, 'Hi.' They were friends, he and his dad; friends and allies.

'How's it been?' His father kept up the geniality. 'Fun?'

'Oh yeah — great.'

'Your mother was saying we should think of other places to meet. You'd be bored with the zoo, she said.'

'Oh no.'

'Actually, she's got a point,' said Penny loyally and more truthfully. 'We do seem to know it all backwards.'

It seemed for a moment that Graham was tempted to take issue with this, but he restrained himself. 'Well, Pen, next time we'll all have a proper discussion about where we spend our time. OK?'

For this, Barbara gave her ex-husband an approving half-smile. He said, 'While you've been doing the rounds, we've been doing a lot of talking.'

You mean arguing, thought Penny. And why does Daddy still call me 'Pen'? Nobody else does. . .except Nick, occasionally.

Barbara took over from Graham. 'And we're not finished talking yet, I'm afraid. It's about Christmas.'

'Yes,' said Graham quickly, 'I was saying that, much as I'd love it if you could both be with me over the holidays, it's not going to be easy this year.'

'When you say "this year",' Barbara said acidly, 'you

mean every year. You've never had them at Christmas. Not even once.'

'I...' He looked blackly at her, conveying very clearly to everyone that it was not his choice to argue in front of his children. 'I simply said,' he continued very slowly, 'that their grandmother was — as ever — very willing to have them. In fact, she'd be heartbroken if they didn't go. That's what I said.'

Barbara adopted his ultra-patient slow-speak. 'And I said, she's not up to it any more. Not with her new hip. She would, of course, *say* she would love to have them, but it wouldn't be true.'

'But you haven't even asked her!'

'No. I've asked you, and you've said "no", you don't want to have your children with you at Christmas.'

'That's not true. I didn't say I didn't *want* them — I said...' He gave up. 'Look, kids, Mum and I really haven't had much of a chance to talk yet — do you think you could wander around for a bit longer? Just a bit longer?'

'Sure — no problem,' said Nick.

Barbara gave Penny a short smile of reassurance; Penny smiled back sympathetically.

As they walked away again, a parrot of some kind began a repetitious screeching and Penny couldn't help but think it echoed the relationship her parents now had. 'I suppose Dad's pretty sick about the Toy Boy,' she said.

'Oh no, he doesn't mind about that. He said, "good luck to her".' Nick omitted to tell Penny the way in which the words had been spoken. He had also claimed the 'Toy Boy' epithet was his own, when in fact it had been his father's expression.

'Anyway,' Penny said, 'it's none of his business now whether Mummy marries again or not — or how old the bloke is.'

'No, but she makes it his business if she wants to swan off on a honeymoon over Christmas.'

'It's not a honeymoon. Tony's got to go and write about

a conference on ecology — it all just fits in, that's all.'

'Yeah? I suppose they'd still get married and swan off even if he had to go to Birmingham and not the West Indies, then.'

'Yes, I suppose they would,' Penny said bluntly.

They made their way towards the area where the big cats were housed. There was another announcement about the missing boy and the whereabouts of the Lost Children's Post. Penny noticed again the general lack of interest in the announcement. It was like when a burglar alarm clanged resoundingly on a shopfront in a crowded street. Everyone just went right on without a second glance. She said, 'What I can't see is why Daddy can't have me over Christmas if he's got to have you anyway.'

'Well. . .we're used to each other. I'm older than you — I can look after myself. He can go out if he has to.'

'Does he?' Penny asked, interested.

'Oh sure. Quite a lot, actually. What you don't seem to understand, Penny, is how hard he works. He's not one of your Green Party do-gooders, sitting around setting the world to rights over cups of dandelion tea.'

'I bet he said that, not you.'

Nick was triumphant. 'Wrong. I just said it, didn't I?'

'He said it first, though.'

'He works really hard. He's having a tough time with the job and we haven't got a car at the moment. It wouldn't be at all convenient for him — really.'

Penny felt unwanted. Which was foolish, because it was not as if she had any great longing to spend Christmas with Nick and her father. She said, 'For someone who thinks he's super-efficient, it's pretty silly Daddy hasn't got a car. Being stuck out there in the country.'

'There's a local taxi, you know. He had a deal going on the car he wanted, but it fell through.'

'What deal?'

Nick had no idea. He said, 'He got a fabulous price on the old one. Mind you, it was a fabulous car.'

Barbara owned a two-door hatchback. Penny quoted her. 'I think it's crazy to spend a fortune for a set of seats on a set of wheels.' She spoke without passion. From their encounters over the last couple of years it was apparent that she and Nick had little common conversational ground. 'How's school?' she asked brightly, like a distant and possibly elderly relative. The pause before Nick answered told her more than his eventual reply.

'Not too bad, thanks. Yours?'

'It's good.'

There was no common ground there, either. Penny went to a state school and Nick to a private boarding school.

'I wish we had long weekends like you do,' Penny said. He had longer holidays, too.

Nick answered with superiority, 'We work harder when we do work.'

Penny doubted it, but did not argue the point. 'It's a form of artificial life, isn't it, school,' she thought aloud. 'They make patterns where there aren't any. Don't you ever long to get out into reality sometimes? I do. Even if it was only working in a shop.'

'And then where would you be? Nowhere. You need qualifications. You need an edge. It's a tough world out there.'

Big talk, thought Penny. Nick would have a difficult time of it at her school if he sounded off like that; he wasn't half as confident as he wanted to appear and that weakness would be cruelly exploited. Perhaps it was — at his school...

She came out of her reverie to find that she was face to face with a tiger.

There was only a metre between them and for the first time she realized how big a big cat could be. She felt a little electric tingle of fright, in her shoulder of all places. Of course the tiger was behind glass; a thick oval window set into the concrete of the beasts' living quarters. Its coat hung slackly over muscle and bone. Didn't animals sense

8

the presence of fear? She was surprised it did not react to her shock; it just went on staring at her with a complete lack of any feeling. It made one uncomfortable to matter so little, to be the subject of that hugely empty gaze. Had there been no glass between them, would it have killed her with the same impersonal regard?

Nick said, 'I wonder how much that glass costs. When you think about it, it must be colossally expensive to run a zoo.'

Because she had been upset by the tiger she was snappy and wanted to hurt. She said, 'You're going to be one of those people who knows the price of everything and the value of nothing.'

He had not heard that one before and she could see him working it out. 'Quite clever, that.' They turned away from the tiger. 'What's this Toy Boy really like, then, eh? Do you see them kissing and holding hands and all that?'

It was his way of trying to hurt her back and, seeing this, Penny chose not to rise to the bait.

'I don't know what he's like at all. He's always trying to be nice to me, so it's impossible to tell.'

Twenty minutes had passed and the voice was still unhurried, unworried.

'Would Christopher Lucas, who is out in the zoo, please make his way to the Lost Children's Post where his parents are waiting for him.'

It had been settled: it was Christmas in Cambridgeshire. Graham had let his children see just how angry he was that Barbara had won the day.

They were leaving the zoo now and, as tended to happen at least once when they all met up, Barbara walked with Nick and Graham walked with Penny.

Graham said, 'I'm sorry if I wasn't very gracious. It doesn't mean I don't love you.' Penny smiled a vague response. 'Listen — we'll have a really good time. It'll be

9

good. We'll get to know each other again. I'm looking forward to it now!'

She hugged herself into him for a moment, since it was probably what he wanted.

'I mean it,' he went on. 'We'll have talks. You can help with the cooking.'

'That's sexist, Daddy.'

'Is it? Well, I suppose it is. But you might come round to it when you see what a terrible cook I am!'

Barbara was saying, 'When we're back we'll arrange something. I know it must all seem very sudden to you, but that's just how things are sometimes. You won't be missing anything at all, not coming to the wedding. It's only a registry office and we're not having a reception.'

You must be funny in the head, Nick thought. He didn't want to go to her wedding — it would be weird — it was nothing to do with him.

'What's she doing now?' his mother said.

Penny had darted away from Graham and was running towards the gift shop. They saw her talking to the grubby T-shirt.

'Where's your jacket?'

'Got ten pence?'

'No. Where's your jacket?'

'I don't know.'

'Is it pale blue?'

'It's rubbish here, isn't it. Specially when you got no money.'

'Well, is it? Is it pale blue?'

'Yeah. I put it down someplace.'

'You're Christopher Lucas, aren't you.'

'Yeah. Who are you?'

'I'm the person who's going to take you to your mum and dad.'

'All right. If you like.'

She took his hand.

Later she felt guilty because Christopher's mother had

been very agitated and had slapped him twice. It had been a nasty scene at the Lost Children's Post.

Later still, she remembered how her father had comforted her and laughed and how he had been quite droll and charming as he said, 'You'll think twice next time, won't you!'

CHAPTER 2

'WHAT DO you reckon?'

'It's not very straight.'

'It'll do, won't it, though?'

'Oh, why not.' Penny was fed up with the whole business.
After he had set up the fold-away synthetic tree, Graham
had promised for days that he would be getting some
things to hang elsewhere; at last, on Christmas Eve itself,
Penny and Nick had walked the half-mile into the village
to find some paper decorations. Even the largest shop they
went into, a tiny supermarket, had no choice at all to offer
at this late stage, and it might as well have been the eve
of a battle and not Christmas: so many people were tetchy
and rude.

Deep purple paper-chains now sagged gravely around
the sitting-room, asking serious Victorian questions of the
designer-abstract pictures which had a more permanent
place on the white walls.

Penny knew her father had engaged a top-notch company
to refurbish the house when he moved in. To her eyes the
operation had not been a success. From the outside, a pair
of nineteenth-century, joined farm cottages and inside,
gutted pale simplicity; a compendium of modern house-
conversion techniques, begging to be featured in a glossy
magazine. The effect was ordered and self-aware: 'Executive
bachelor self-cleaning dwelling for the discriminating
high-earner.'

The farm the cottages had been a part of had long ago
been swallowed up by a much larger estate. Hedgerows
and trees had been uprooted in the pursuit of ever-larger
fields, so that great tracts of land dedicated to wheat and

barley sprawled across the flat, flat countryside as far as the eye could see. It was as if a crazed cosmetic surgeon had sedated his patient beyond protest and had carefully, one by one, cut away every single distinguishing feature.

You could keep Cambridgeshire, Penny thought. This part of it, anyway. And these twin cottages with their hearts torn out, too.

'You don't look very happy,' Nick said, stepping down from the chair he had been standing on.

'It's so *boring* here.'

'In my day we used to make our own amusements.'

'Isn't that witty.'

'Do you want a go on the computer? Dad might let you, if you asked.'

'No. He's busy.'

Graham had spent much of their time together in his neon-lit study, working, 'because I have to, to make up time I've lost through being here with you.' So he wasn't with them much. So what was the point of his taking these days off in the first place?

He worked in Research and Development for a communications company, though what that meant Penny had no idea, except that it was stressful and time-consuming. She had a suspicion that Nick didn't know too much about it either, even if he did claim to be his father's confidant in all things. However, she might be underestimating her brother here, because he was pretty technically-minded.

'Snooker,' he now said. 'What about that, then?'

'No thank you very much,' Penny answered politely.

'You'll never learn if you don't try.'

'It's not worth learning anyway.'

She had found that a hazard of staying with Nick was his constant determination to drag her into the annexe at the side of the house, there to deal out crushing defeats on the three-quarter size snooker table that was his obsession.

With her father shut away fiddling with his computer and Nick practising stun shots on the other side of the .

house, Penny was beginning to feel invisible; that old feeling she used to have when her mother was occupied with adult friends.

'Well, I'm going to pot a few balls,' Nick announced, wandering to the door. He looked back. 'Looks awful, doesn't it.' He meant the decorations.

'Yes.'

'Oh, well...'

She heard his footsteps on the wooden floor of the hall, gathering pace the second he was out of the room and on his way to the annexe.

Penny slumped down on the sofa. It was impossible not to feel resentful towards her mother for dumping her here while she jetted off into the sunset with her young man. This rising bitterness was unwelcome. She had wanted Barbara to be happy. Now it was clear to her how disturbed she was by the interloper, Tony, whom her mother — her *mother* — had surrendered to, becoming helpless with love... Ugh.

'Tony' was such a pathetic name, too. And that was fine, because Tony was pathetic. Steel-rimmed tinted spectacles and springy fair hair and a lot of intense talk about the hidden international issues... Pretentious, and quite obviously pretending when he demonstrated his concern about Penny's feelings and her well-being... Enough.

Enough. It was a stony problem beyond resolution; consistently ugly no matter how often you circled it or tried to wrestle it to a more pleasing form. The one ray of sunshine, sitting here now, was that it was a problem that had quite literally gone away for a while.

Her only real concern at this moment was how to occupy her time. She wondered where Graham had hidden his presents for them and what they were. She herself expected no heartfelt thanks for her own presents to her father and brother: a silk tie for Graham and for Nick, *The Guinness Book of Records*. Barbara had said, 'It's impossible, choosing

14

presents for men.' Penny remembered that she had then smiled secretly, thinking affectionately of the Toy Boy, no doubt, and the impending wedding.

Yes — the quiet wedding... The formalities at the Registry Office had been short and to the point, like last-minute instructions from a referee at a sporting encounter. Only Penny and her grandmother had been present and the old lady might well have missed the entire ceremony, so preoccupied was she with some worry about her hip.

And then, with (one could say) the full weight of the law now behind him, Tony kissed her mother...

Oh dear. Back on that. Penny went over to the television and turned it on. The sound preceded the picture.

'...Great Carpet Giveaway! Starts Boxing Day!'

The picture arrived. A man in an unconvincing blazer was disseminating the good news in a warehouse piled high with rolls of carpeting. He was as awestruck as if he had been witness to the arrival of the baby Jesus.

'Unbelievable selection of top-quality names! Low-cost credit available!'

Penny switched off the set and went to the window.

Outside the land rolled away to the horizon like a brown sea. The sky was almost equally featureless, a stained grey like the blade of an old kitchen knife. Didn't time fly when you were having fun. Christmas Eve morning and it felt like a slow Sunday. Oh well, perhaps today her father might let her have a go on the computer after all... He might even teach her some of its tricks if he had the time...

It was so quiet in the house that she could hear the intermittent 'click' of ball hitting ball on the snooker table. No noise from the study: good, the computer wasn't in use then.

The study door was ajar and she opened it noiselessly because the silence held the suggestion that her father might be asleep.

He had his head in his hands, with his elbows resting heavily on the desk in front of the computer screen. From where she stood at the door, Penny could see that the screen was filled with rows of numbers. She could make out the heading, '4 × 13: Classic Non-Predictive Chaotic Sequences.'

'Daddy?'

As he turned he tapped on the keyboard and the screen went blank.

'Hi.'

'Hello, Daddy.'

'What's up?'

'Nothing.' She was tempted to add, 'That's the trouble.'

'Where's Nick?'

'Snookering.'

'Selfish through and through, isn't he.'

'You're working, then...'

'That's what I do in here, I'm afraid. Bad news if you're looking for company.'

'Is it very secret, your work?'

'It is, actually. Well, it has to be a secret from the competition, anyway.'

'Ah.'

'Just a reflex action, switching it off.'

'I see.'

'I bet there's lots on the telly.'

He was beginning to get twitchy, she saw. He had been on edge ever since she had arrived and it was hard not to believe she was the cause of it, though Nick had assured her that this was not the case. Apparently Graham was working on a vital contract that could either make or break his career with the company. It all sounded very melodramatic, but what would she know about it, coming from a home where they seemed to know no one who worked in business.

Penny lingered in the doorway. It would be interesting to have a go on the computer. At home, her mother tapped out her occasional magazine articles on an old portable typewriter.

'Could you get out now?' Her father spoke sharply and she could see little muscles tightening around his mouth. 'I am extremely busy, you know.'

She felt a sudden rush of emotion which expanded low down in her throat so that she could not speak.

Graham said, 'I'm sorry...I'm sorry.' He wasn't, so he repeated it, trying to mean it this time. 'I'm *sorry*.'

Penny managed to swallow. 'It doesn't matter.'

He did not come to her as her mother would have. 'Well, it does. I didn't want to snap at you. It's just a bad time for me, that's all. The work's not coming along as it should.'

Now he stood up, fiddling with the signet ring he wore. 'The fact is, I may have to go into work today.' He looked at Penny almost defiantly. She wasn't protesting but he held up his hands as if she was. 'I know, I know — it's Christmas Eve. I know. I'll make it up to you. Believe me, I didn't plan it like this, but there're some things I can only do at work.' He took a deep breath. 'It's possible I'll be back extremely late.'

This time he gave her a good chance to speak, but again she had nothing to say.

'Sorry. Nick knows the form. I'd better shave...'

Having made the decision he was all action, striding past her out of the room, calling, 'Nick? Nicky?'

It was strange how joyous he sounded all at once, as though a great burden had been lifted from him. 'Nick? Can you call Countrywide Cars for me? I've got to go to the station.'

Well, at least someone was happy. 'Men are like children,' Barbara was fond of saying. Maybe. And maybe she just wanted them to be, which was why she had chosen a younger man for her new husband...

Shut up. Shut up.

'Can you turn it down a little, Nick?'

'Why?'

Cartoon spacecraft corkscrewed across the television screen, zapping out cartoon laser beams. The evil spacecraft exploded at regular intervals, while in the other type of craft all the good guys survived but looked very tense.

'*Bandit on our tail, Commander!*' *WHEE, SWAATCH!* '*Got him!*'

'Do turn it down.'

'You don't get it, do you. This is a cult show — you have the sound up loud for this.'

'I can't see it makes it any better,' Penny shouted above the fury of the space battle.

'Then you're a bore, then, aren't you.'

'You should think about other people.'

'What other people? There aren't any neighbours, you know.'

'Well think about me, then.'

She went to turn down the sound. Nick was quite happy just to argue.

'Think about you? Why? I don't stop you doing what you want to do.'

'There's nothing here I do want to do.'

'Oh dear,' he mocked. 'Well, I'm afraid there isn't any wool anywhere, if you want to knit. That's what old women do, isn't it? Knit?'

'If I can do what I want to do, why can't we watch something else?'

'You didn't want to watch anything else.'

He looked beaky and spiteful. A rude stranger.

'I do now,' she said patiently.

'Your turn later.'

He walked over and turned the volume up full blast. WHEEE — BLAP!

The guest bedroom had an especially impersonal atmosphere. Like a hotel room it was designed to offend no one, whatever their taste.

18

Graham had persuaded Nick to lend Penny his radio-cassette player and now she had it on very quietly to keep her company. It was not that she was being considerate in keeping the noise down: she had no intention of giving Nick the satisfaction of knowing she was using his expensive possession.

He had called her an old woman. It wasn't true. It was only the way she reacted to him: she was fine with everyone else. Wasn't she...? What was the time? She looked at her cheap digital watch. Nearly three o'clock. Nick's watch was water resistant to two hundred metres. Perhaps Graham had given him a scuba-diving outfit to go with it. It wouldn't surprise her. She heard her mother saying, 'We have all we need. To most people in the world, that is riches. Think about it.' Oh sure, all well and good, but it was only of any comfort when you thought about poor people. If your own brother was better off than you it was rather different.

She hoisted herself off the bed and walked out on to the landing. Now the television downstairs was relaying the film *Mary Poppins*. It had been going for a while. 'Oh, it's a jolly holiday with Mary...'

Penny knelt at the top of the stairs and called down. 'Nick! Should we ring...' she hesitated '... Daddy?'

'Why?' Nick shouted back.

'Well, I mean—supper. When do we have it?'

'When we want it,' called back her brother's disembodied voice.

'Won't we have it with him? Why don't we telephone and find out when he's coming back?'

'You don't telephone him at work. House rule. *Never.*'

It would be quite nice to see *Mary Poppins* again. Penny stayed kneeling at the top of the stairs for a few seconds longer.

Then she went back into the guest bedroom.

* * *

19

The sky was the charcoal grey of a sober business suit and Nick was playing snooker again.

Sitting on the sofa downstairs, Penny could hear the murmur of a fantasized commentary.

'Oh, that's a truly remarkable shot. But he's not on the black quite as he'd like to be. . .'

How childish. In her hands Penny held a Fodor guide to France. There was nothing to read here; nothing of any interest to her. It was all business stuff and the kind of thrillers that pictured combinations of lips, guns and money on their front covers. Finally she had taken down the travel book with the half-hearted notion of broadening her knowledge about another country.

The words jumped about on the pages and refused to be read.

By common consent, supper was taken early.

Refusing all offers of help, Nick bustled around the gleaming kitchen showing how practised he was at looking after himself. His cooking was strictly 'heat-according-to-instructions-on-packet'; in this instance fish fingers, potato waffles and peas.

The neon lights above the fitted cupboards reflected against the blackness beyond the windows. Penny had toyed with the idea of pulling down the brilliant yellow blinds, but to do so would be to emphasize that she and Nick were in a way imprisoned here in the cottage, so she stayed where she was at the pinewood table and watched moths in their winter woollen jackets bumping against the glass.

She started as a clumsy armoured insect cracked against the glass and vanished immediately.

'Eh. . .*voilà!*' Nick put down the plate in front of her.

The food was as the day had been: boring and in endless quantity, and they disposed of it with as much relish as if they had been levelling earth on a building site.

Some hours later, the fare on television was proving equally indigestible.

Two comics went through a series of sketches with one grinning at the other, who acted shy and helpless. Penny and Nick were not in the mood for it.

With the whole sofa to herself, Penny sat neatly on the edge of the cushions. Nick was sprawled full-length on the carpet, close to the television.

At this moment the comics were in a sketch where the shy one was a householder in pyjamas and the grinning one was Father Christmas. The joke was that Father Christmas had got very drunk on all the little nips of drink left out for him and now fell around shouting about how he detested children. Every now and then Nick would laugh shortly to show he was quicker on the uptake than the studio audience.

The telephone rang.

Nick was on his feet at once.

'I'll get it.'

He almost ran out of the room, with Penny close behind. In the hall they diverged smartly, like a formation dance team. Nick hurried to the study where the cordless phone was kept and Penny went on to the kitchen, where a second phone hung on the wall by the back door. When she got the phone to her ear Nick was already speaking.

'No, we're fine, Dad — fine. No worries here.'

Then her father's voice, sounding strained. 'Good. That's...that's good...' She could hear that he was breathing fast.

Nick again. 'What's the score, Dad? Will you be back soon?'

'Ah...'

'Are you still at the office?'

'Ah... No. No — actually I'm in London.'

'Oh.'

'Had to get down here in a rush. Last minute thing.'

'Oh. I see...'

21

'I was the only one who could, um — who could ...'

Penny wanted to ask 'Could what?' but having failed to speak sooner she now somehow felt that she could take no part in the conversation.

Nick said, 'That's OK, Dad. So when do we expect you?'

Graham's voice became higher, as if it had been stretched. 'Look, Nick, I'm dreadfully sorry.'

A pause. Nick said, 'What do you mean? What about?'

'I'm sorry. I... I've got these clients with me. That's what it is, you see. I've been delegated to entertain them and, uh ...'

He's making it up, Penny thought with disbelief. Yet Nick only said, 'Oh, that's tough luck. You always get the short straw, don't you.'

'I'm sorry.' In those two mumbled words Penny heard an almost childish guilt and she suddenly understood that their father was used to playing on Nick's sympathy in this way. Nick's instant assumption of an adult kind of confidence confirmed this.

'Oh well. Can't be helped. I suppose we won't see you until tomorrow, then.'

Graham became quite incoherent. 'Oh... Uh... Oh God... I don't, um...' Then it seemed he pulled himself together. 'There's tons of stuff in the freezer, isn't there?'

'Yes — tons — but...'

'Good. Just...just do whatever you want to. You'll be fine, won't you. I know you will.'

'Yes, but...'

'Yes. Look — I've got to go now.'

Just like that. He hung up.

There was a gap of some seconds before Nick disengaged the cordless phone. Penny put the kitchen telephone back on its cradle. When she turned round, Nick was in the doorway. 'Listening, were you?'

'Yes.'

For some reason he was angry. 'That's a pretty nasty habit, isn't it.'

22

'It's not a habit. Anyway, he's my father too.'

He glared at her. Penny spoke again. 'What's wrong with him?'

'Wrong with him? Nothing. What do you mean?'

'Something's wrong.'

'I'll tell you what's wrong — they take advantage of him at work — that's what's wrong.'

'He's not working today. Come on — it's Christmas. No one's working. He might have gone to a party... He sounded strange.'

Now Nick was furious. 'He hasn't gone to a party! He wouldn't leave us here!'

'He has left us here.'

'Not for that, he wouldn't. He...he just wouldn't.'

'Then he's in some sort of trouble.'

They looked at one another. Nick shrugged uneasily and walked into the hall. Penny followed.

'It can't be normal, just to take off like that.'

'It is here.'

'Then I think it's dreadful of him. Dreadful for you, too.'

'No it isn't. We have a great time. We've got it all sorted.'

There was no getting through to him. In the sitting-room he stood looking at the television. Penny walked past him and turned off the set.

She said, 'I don't know what Mummy would say.'

Nick wagged his head from side to side and imitated someone much younger. 'Oh, don't you? You don't know what Mumsy would say? I'll tell you — she'd say it was dreadful, quite, quite dreadful.'

'What are we going to *do*?'

'We'll have a good time — don't worry about *that*,' he said in his normal voice. 'We'll open presents and wear party hats and it'll all be fine. Dad'll call again, don't worry.'

He didn't seem very convinced. They looked around at the dismal decorations. He brightened. 'Actually, we ought to find the presents — where he put them. Dad gets terrific things, you know.'

23

'Yeah, I know,' Penny said with a tinge of resentment. 'Yeah, you wait...'

At first the search was quite simply the most entertaining thing that had happened all day. Every cupboard was ransacked, including the linen cupboard. Every article of furniture was moved, every drawer opened, throughout the house.

Nick began to sing his father's praises. 'He is crafty, isn't he. Dead cunning.'

A moment's inspiration suggested the garden shed: a good place if the presents were big! In the dark, stumbling across the dank garden with a torch, Nick giggled.

'Yeah, this is it! Must be!'

Unless Graham had in mind a gift of some old seed packets or a very mobile and hairy spider, it wasn't.

Eventually they came back to the study, where they had started. It was by now nearly midnight and Nick's jollity had evaporated. They stood in the middle of the small room, reduced to thinking instead of looking, now.

'You thought they might be big, didn't you...' Penny mused.

'I wouldn't have been surprised.'

'But what if they were the opposite—really tiny.'

'Well, like what?'

'A ring, say, for me, and—oh, I don't know—just think "tiny".'

They went through their father's desk again. It was an imitation of a pre-war roll-top bureau, finished in smart matt black.

Her eyes sharpened by their long search, Penny noticed how many brown, windowed envelopes the rows of cubbyholes held. The unease she had felt during Graham's phone call returned with vigour.

'Nothing, nothing, nothing!' Nick said angrily, slamming shut the bureau.

'Perhaps he's got them with him. I think you chipped the desk just then.'

'No, he wouldn't take them into the office, would he? He'd have bought them earlier, obviously.'

'If he did buy any.'

'Well, of course he did!'

The thought involuntarily escaped Penny: 'Perhaps if we read his mail, we might get some idea of what's going on.'

The change of subject took Nick by surprise. When he understood, he was cross again. 'No! You don't read people's letters! Like you don't listen to other people's phone calls — though, of course, that wouldn't bother *you!*'

Looking about her, Penny said, 'He hasn't got many Christmas cards, has he?'

'He's not interested in that sort of thing.'

'Hasn't he got lots of friends — at work and so on?'

'I don't know.'

Their eyes met and Nick's slid away. He had been caught out.

He doesn't know much at all, Penny thought; not half as much as he pretends to.

'I'm going to bed,' Nick said abruptly.

'Wait.' Penny caught his arm. 'There aren't any presents. Face it. He didn't get us any presents.'

Nick thought about it. 'Lot on his mind,' he muttered.

'Don't give me that. Something's terribly wrong — something's gone wrong for him. All right, perhaps he genuinely has got a lot on his plate — but whatever it is, you don't know anything about it, do you? Not one tiny thing.' He pulled away from her. 'You don't know any more than I do.' She was contemptuous. 'And he's your big friend.'

'Well, he is. Presents aren't everything.'

'Oh, that's good — coming from you, with everything you've got.'

Yet it was precisely this absence of Christmas presents which was unsettling Penny now. It was quite against the order of things. 'We should call someone,' she said.

'Who?'

'*I* don't know. Who is there around here? Hasn't he got any friends?'

'Not in the village.'

'What about calling someone from his work, then?'

'*No!* We couldn't.' He was aghast. 'I mean — supposing — just supposing — something really is wrong — we couldn't let anyone at the firm know — we couldn't go behind his back like that.'

'So you're not quite sure either, then, that he really is in London on work.'

'Well, he probably *is*, but. . .I think we should just. . .leave it all to him.'

'What about you? Isn't there someone you'd like to call?'

He put on a world-weary act. 'Oh, come off it, Penny. We can't ring anyone up now — it's midnight.'

'All right. Tomorrow. Who will you call?'

Silence.

'There must be someone you talk to.'

'Well. . .not here.'

'You haven't got any friends?'

'I said — not here!'

She was surprised and intrigued. 'At school, though — you've got friends at school?'

Through Nick's mind there passed the urge to tell her the truth: a simple 'no'. His silence said it anyway.

'Oh, Nick.'

Nick squirmed. She was sorry for him. This was appalling. His shabby little sister was sorry for him. And there was no reason for it — they were happy enough, he and his dad. They had a great time together. . . He felt his eyes begin to prickle.

'I'm going to bed.'

'You can't — we've got to think of someone we can call tomorrow!'

'Well, I suppose there's always Eric,' he said tiredly.

'Great. Good. We'll call Eric, then. Who's Eric?'

'He's just the gardener.' He changed his mind, then.

'No—he'd be useless. He's just a chap who helps out in the garden. Hopeless.'

Irrationally, it was Nick's apparent contempt for the hired help that opened the floodgates of Penny's churning emotions. They poured themselves into this one narrow channel with enormous energy.

'That's absolutely typical! You're so spoilt! You've got no feelings for people! He's just the gardener so he can't help! Just a *servant*, is he?'

Nick took a step towards her and shouted back, 'He's hopeless! You don't understand!'

'Yes I do! Daddy pays him so you despise him! It's just that simple! You should have respect for every single person on this earth—we're all equal, in case you didn't know!' Somewhere deep beneath the uproar of feelings Penny recognized her mother's ideas in this. She went right on. 'But you wouldn't know anything about that, because you think you're above it all—better than other people!'

'You're so simplistic,' Nick jeered.

'That's just jargon!'

'No—it's true—you don't see things as they are. Some people are, um, instigators and motivators and others are more like—what is it?—worker bees! We're not equal at all! Oh yes, you might start with equal opportunities, in a perfect world, but you wouldn't end up with everyone equal—never! Can't you see that? Some people don't even *want* to be equal.'

'I don't believe I'm hearing this! It's just second-hand garbage—and I know who you got it from!'

'Oh, sure—I know you don't like Dad!'

Penny shrieked out, 'I don't know him—how can I dislike him?'

That effectively collapsed the argument. They both took the chance to get some air into their lungs.

Then Penny said quietly, 'So we'll call this Eric, then—all right? He might know a little something about what's been going on — he might have been told something.'

Nick began to laugh. He was exhausted and the laughter shook his whole body. 'I'm going to bed.'

Penny shouted, 'We've got to talk!'

He was going up the stairs. 'We have talked. And I've had enough of it.'

'Well, so have I!'

It was an empty rejoinder, spoken without thought in order to have the last word. Penny took a last long look at the room before she left it to go up to the guest bedroom. She was tired, too...

They would have to take some kind of action tomorrow. Anything was better than just hanging about here for hour after hour.

She turned off the light and went upstairs in the dark. It was all wrong here and Nick just laughed.

CHAPTER 3

IN THE utter blackness of the early morning, Penny's first thought on waking was, 'It's Christmas!'

A compound of memories and expectations burst in her like a sky-rocket. As with the firework, the colours flared and shrivelled and fell to earth as cinders. She was in the cottage. The feel of the lightweight duvet was different to hers at home; remembrance of the friendly smells of her own bedroom (dust and femininity) was overwhelmed by a bland, clean smell that might have been wallpaper paste.

Penny groped for the unfamiliar bedside light and felt her way down the flex to the switch. Immediately, she shut her eyes against the glare that bounced off the glass top of the bedside table.

She didn't feel like moving again. She'd just lie here with her arm over her eyes until...No. There was a reason why she should get up. She had to take a good look at Graham's study, because it was all wrong here. She swung out of bed and her foot hit something.

It was a present; a rectangle which had been expensively wrapped in reflecting silver and green paper, with a silver ribbon tied perfectly around it. Perhaps it was the sudden motion as she sat up, or perhaps it was relief that made Penny dizzy for a second.

He was back. He had come back in the early hours and everything was back on course for a normal Christmas.

And he did, too, buy the most marvellous presents...

The thought that she should postpone the opening of the gift passed through without stopping. By brute force she pulled and elongated the ribbon until she was able to tear at the wrapping. The present did not reveal itself easily: it had been gift-wrapped in an expensive shop, no doubt about that. She tore a nail in the struggle to reach the inner glories. . .

. . .A box of cheap bath-salts. The kind of present you could buy twice; once for her and once for her grandmother. Well, thanks a lot, Daddy. Listlessly she reached for and read the glittering gift-tag. 'Penny from Nick.' No 'Happy Christmas'; no 'love', just bath-salts dressed as diamonds by an indulgent shop assistant. . . From Nick, not her father.

He wasn't back. Last night's anxiety snapped back into place as if she had not slept at all.

Penny discovered that she was burning with anger. Had she been truthful with herself, it was the tawdry present that had triggered it, yet it hardly mattered once she had focused the rage on Graham. He was criminally irresponsible and uncaring, staying away like this. She would take great pleasure in rooting about amongst his private correspondence until she discovered a clue as to what it was he was up to.

She threw the present on to the bed and marched to the door.

Then she went back for her dressing-gown. While it was mild for the time of year, it was none too warm. 'Be practical,' she told herself.

She went down the stairs as quietly as she could.

Nick lay in bed looking up at the ceiling by the light of his torch. The interior decorator had fought a losing battle with a damp patch up there and if you could look long enough and without thinking of anything, a sepia skull-shape would appear in the stains, with a point of evil light in one eye socket. Yes, there it was. It would take a truly gifted artist to get that effect, Nick thought.

He heard Penny tiptoeing down the stairs. Stupid kid. Probably she'd be one of those people who liked to tell you exactly how much longer than you they had been up. Or awake.

He turned off the torch. When would Dad get back this time? It was worrying. Not because anything would have happened to him. No. You could trust Dad. 'I want a completely adult relationship, Nick,' his father had said. 'Total trust on both sides.' And that's what they had and it was great. Still, it would be hard to tell a stranger — which was virtually what Penny was — that he was used to being left alone here for really pretty long periods of time. Two whole days and nights, on occasion.

'I work hard, Nicky. I need to enjoy myself from time to time. They call it rest and recreation.'

The worrying thing was that it was Christmas...Dad just wouldn't waltz off at Christmas or on a birthday unless he really had to. If that had been the case, the adult relationship thing required that Nick be informed about it rather more fully than by one short, garbled phone call. So...Dad was in trouble and it must be about work. That was the only conclusion one could reach. He'd make it up to Nick, though — to both his children. He always did.

Could it be a woman? Nick was fairly sure his dad had a woman in his life. In London, probably. Probably looked like one of those girls in the commercials. Smart and sophisticated. She wouldn't want to marry Dad. They would have an adult relationship of another kind — a casual kind of thing.

But it wasn't a woman this time, at Christmas. It was that awful job again, which caused his father so much tension. Nothing one could do — the rules were, you waited and trusted and everything would be all right.

'Loyalty is a old-fashioned virtue, Nick. It's all I ask of you.'

Yes...he'd wait. Although not with Penny until he had to. She had a trick of getting under your skin and making you think things you didn't want to think. When all the time you knew it was that dreadful job again.

He wondered if Penny had opened her present yet. She must have, but she hadn't looked in to thank him. Well, he wasn't surprised.

Nick looked at the luminous hands of his watch. Seven

o'clock. OK—when he got downstairs he'd tell her he'd been awake from five thirty. He turned over on to his side and went to sleep.

The floor of the study was covered with paper. On a normal Christmas the paper would be tissue and gift-wrapping: here there were neat rows of bills, bank statements and correspondence.

Penny was so absorbed that she had left the lights on, though it was light by now; a cool, neutral kind of day. She was trying to keep cool and neutral herself, but her heart was beating quickly and she felt that sort of weakness that comes from the need for food, specifically sugar.

She was standing with her arms folded, staring at one particular letter on the floor.

'What are you *doing!*'

Nick was in the doorway, outraged in his pyjamas. 'What do you think you're *doing!*'

'Calm down, Nick.'

Of course, that made matters worse. 'You can't do this—it's dishonest! It's...it's a betrayal of trust!' His voice was shrill. 'How dare you. How *dare* you! Put them back—now!'

Penny kept her own voice low. 'I want you to see what I've seen, Nick.'

'No...no!' He was frantic. 'Put them back! How dare you!'

He knelt down and began gathering up pieces of paper.

'No, Nick—I had it all ordered.'

'You're disgusting!'

'Don't do it, Nick!'

She bent down and grabbed at the papers in his hand. Nick shoved backwards at her, violently, and she sat down, disarranging more of her careful work. Her brother wildly swept up whole rows of the letters. Penny jumped on his back. 'No, Nick—you don't understand!' Now she was as angry as he was.

He stood up with Penny still clinging to his shoulders and reeled towards the desk. Penny dragged her feet on the carpet and used both hands to steer him away from his objective. He pulled away from her and she caught at his forearm and swung him around with such force that he fell over, dropping the papers.

He rolled over and jumped up and came at her, making small involuntary noises of distress and fury, the papers forgotten.

'No — listen — Nick!'

He launched himself at her and they crashed to the floor with Nick punching at her arms and shoulders. In a panic to get away, Penny elbowed him in the face and Nick punched harder. She clasped him in a bear-hug and they rolled over and over, crushing letters and envelopes.

'You...you...!' Nick panted.

'He's been sacked!' Penny shouted. The last word coincided with Nick's full weight rolling on to her, so that it shot out on her breath like an exclamation of despair. 'He doesn't have a job any more!'

They rolled over one last time and the fight ceased. Nick extricated himself from Penny's manic embrace. They were both trembling.

'What?' Nick said.

'He hasn't been telling you the truth. He's lost his job. Look — it's here somewhere...' She began to sort through the papers. 'No, not that one...'

Nick sat back and watched her. Now it came to it, he hardly needed to see the proof in writing. It had to be true. And when it was faced, at last, there was a measure of relief, because so much of his father's recent bursts of temper and swings of emotion could be explained by it.

Instinctively, Nick began to erect new defences for Graham. He, Nick, had not been told because Dad had not wanted to worry him. It wasn't that Nick had been lied to: he had been protected, by his loving father. He looked out of the window. It was Christmas Day, wasn't it. . .? He couldn't like Penny for this. She was probably loving every moment, wasn't she. Little cow.

In fact, Penny was experiencing little emotion as she searched for the vital letter. She felt vindicated and tremendously efficient, that was all. If only Nick had listened for a moment — she'd had it all laid out. Ah. Here it was.

'Here,' she said crisply. 'Look.'

She passed over a bent sheet of grey notepaper. Nick saw the company's heading and the signature at the bottom: James Sheridan, Managing Director. Nick read the letter and passed it back without a word. With no consideration for his feelings, Penny then proceeded to read him a passage from the letter, narrowing her eyes shrewdly as if she were Sherlock Holmes and he the plodding Dr Watson.

' "Under the circumstances a redundancy settlement of any description would be inappropriate." What does that suggest to you?'

'Shut up, Penny,' he said listlessly.

'What it suggests to me is a major bust-up. He never gave you a single hint about this, did he?'

Nick shrugged as if he didn't care.

'And did you notice the date?'

He took some interest now. 'No. Give it to me.' He snatched back the letter.

'July the fourth,' Penny said remorselessly.

Nick got up, suddenly very restless. July. Before the summer holidays. A long, long time ago. Months of deceit.

'Independence Day,' was all he said.

'What?'

'American Independence Day. July the fourth. . .'

'Oh.' She was confused.

'What else did you find?'

'Unpaid bills. Bank statements. I couldn't really work those out, except he's got no money, I don't think. There's a letter from your school.'

'Oh yes?'

She was embarrassed for him. 'They haven't been paid for two terms.'

'I see.'

'There's a couple of letters from people at work — sorry he's leaving. You get the impression it was sudden and they didn't know why.'

'You've been very thorough, haven't you.'

'And there's a few from Mummy, too, I'm afraid. About money.'

Without in the least raising his voice Nick said, 'Get out, Penny. Get out of here.'

'I'll show you — and he's in trouble with his credit cards, too.'

'No. Just get out. This is his room. This is my house.' He wasn't angry but he meant it none the less.

'Some of the bills — it's a wonder we haven't been cut off.'

'No, Penny — that's enough. I'll have a look myself, if you don't mind. Just leave me alone for a bit. OK?'

In the face of this strange, courteous behaviour, she found she could not continue with her grisly list of findings. She felt both guilty, and unaccountably angry again. With herself, this time. Though really she had acted very sensibly... She opened her mouth to say this; shut it, and left the room quietly.

Her last impression was of Nick kneeling motionless amidst the scattered papers.

While she waited for her brother in the sitting-room, Penny pretended to read the guide to France. She had the feeling that if she was caught watching television it would somehow seem uncaring.

After a long time, she was conscious that Nick had joined her in the room. He came and sat down beside her on the sofa.

'Well...' he said.

Penny kept a tactful silence.

'Well.' Some energy came back into his voice. 'It's quite

a mess. I've got most of it sorted, I think.' As Penny had been, he was proud of feeling responsible and efficient. 'There's a couple of interesting things. He gets money from somewhere. Every time a bill comes due you find he puts enough money in his account to cover it. Until recently.'

'I hadn't spotted that,' Penny said humbly.

'Did you see about the flat?'

'No, I don't think so. There were a few things I was going to come back to. I was trying to do it in some kind of sequence — you know — um. . .'

'Chronologically.'

'Yes.'

'Ah.' He was pleased he knew something she didn't. 'Well, two months ago he became the owner of a place in London. On a mortgage. He had to take out a mortgage on this place too, to afford the down payment. So his outgoings got totally out of hand.'

'I see.' Penny didn't, quite.

'So probably he's been spending quite a lot of time in London.'

'Yes, but why? If he didn't have a job?'

'That's the big question.'

'Perhaps he has got some sort of job. He worked away for hours on the computer.'

'I thought of that. The trouble is, if Dad doesn't want you to see data, you won't see it. I tried, believe me. He's wicked on a computer.'

It was impossible not to feel the old pride for his father. It made Nick feel all the more betrayed.

'I don't know what to do,' he said shakily.

'Nor do I.'

'He could have told me. He could have told me anything. I'm on his side, whatever happened.'

'Mmn,' said Penny non-committally. 'Is there a telephone number for this flat?'

Nick recovered himself. 'No. I tried Directory Enquiries, too.'

36

'He could be there, do you think?'

'It's the only place we know he might be at.'

'But there's no phone.' She waited for a while and then said casually, 'I've got a number for Mummy upstairs. In my diary. For emergencies.'

'No! No!' He sprang up. 'Absolutely not. It wouldn't be fair.'

'Who to?' she asked with feeling.

'To Dad. He's never let me down — not once. He'll come through — I know he will.'

She couldn't help sounding smug. 'Come through what? That's the point, isn't it? He hasn't told you what's going on in his life. He's been lying to you.'

'You shut up! You're talking about my father!'

They were back to confrontation. Penny stood up, too. 'He's made a fool of you and you defend him. You're hopeless. What do you think people would say if they knew we'd been left alone here?'

'If you tell anyone, I'll kill you!'

'Oh, fine. That would just solve everything, wouldn't it.'

'Where are you going?' He was in a panic, fearing she might be going to a telephone.

'To my room.' She just had to add, bitterly, 'Oh — Happy Christmas, by the way.'

Upstairs, Penny felt like crying without quite knowing why, except that her situation must surely justify it for once.

She sat on the bed and picked up her Christmas present from Nick. She mustn't give in to tears. She had to have control of herself in order to have some control over what happened. She lay back. It was foolish to antagonize Nick, she knew. That wouldn't help either of them. . .

Penny fell asleep, still clutching the despised box of bath salts.

When Nick knocked on the door an hour later, Penny woke up with that instant and absurd compulsion to deny that one has been asleep at all. 'Hello?' she said quickly and with quite brilliant vivacity.

'It's Nick,' came a dull voice.

'Sure — come in.' She hastily put the bath salts aside and lowered her feet to the floor.

He came in. 'Sorry I keep shouting.'

'That's OK.'

He noticed the bath salts.

'Sorry about your present.'

'That's OK. Oh — I've got one for you too.'

She drew out her case from under the bed and took out a package which had been wrapped in kitchen foil, not very well.

He took it. 'Thanks.'

'Open it, then.'

'Right.' He sat on the bed and pulled off the kitchen foil. He didn't open the book. '*Guinness Book of Records.* Thanks.'

'There's some snooker stuff in it. Highest scores and stuff.'

'Thanks.'

'Sorry.'

'No, it's interesting,' he said with the same dull voice.

'What are we going to do?' Penny asked.

He stood up. 'We're going to have lunch. I've put the turkey in already.'

It was hard to carve the pale, partially-cooked bird.

'I followed the instructions on the wrapper,' Nick said defensively.

'There's more goodness in it if it isn't cooked to a cinder.'

'Well it certainly isn't that.'

The roast potatoes, on the other hand, had absorbed incredible quantities of heat and crumbled like charcoal. Nick said, 'I couldn't be bothered with the pudding.'

Afterwards he suggested a game of cards: piquet, which he and Graham used to play together. Since it was apparently hard to learn and she didn't much want to play anything anyway, Penny refused the offer.

Instead, Nick brought down a board game which they set out on the kitchen table, where their unfinished food still lay. The game advertised itself as 'a journey through life with infinite variations' — which all concerned how much money you earned or lost as you went round the board.

Penny read out from a card, ' "Pedestrian sues you after car accident. Pay five thousand pounds or gamble on outcome of case." '

Nick gambled, lost and paid double. 'Your go.'

Penny took up the dice. 'I don't like it here — just us.'

'A five. You can buy unit trusts if you want, where you are now.'

'I'm scared, Nick. We don't know what's happened to him.'

He moved her counter, a car. 'They're not worth it anyway, unit trusts.'

'Anything could have happened. Like a car accident, for instance.'

'He hasn't got a car, has he?' Nick said savagely. He rattled the dice and threw. 'One.'

'Other people have cars. Pedestrians do get hit.'

'Don't be stupid.'

'We shouldn't be here by ourselves,' she insisted.

'So you keep saying. It doesn't bother me.'

'It's not as safe as it used to be — anywhere. That's what Mummy says. There's funny people around.'

He flicked her car off the board. 'Oh dear. Hurricane force winds. You're dead. I couldn't care less what your Mummy says.'

She had to say it. 'I think we should call the police.'

Penny thought he was going to throw the whole board across the room, then. He controlled himself with a great effort and grasped the sides of the table very tightly.

'You haven't thought it out at all, have you.' He looked very white in the face. 'Dad was in a state when he called.

OK — I admit it — he's never sounded like that before. Well, if he's so hard up, had it occurred to you that he might have been getting his money by doing something illegal? He could be, you know. And you want to call the police!'

'Oh.' The word came out short and sharp like the jolt of shock that had just hit her.

'We've got to wait until he comes back or until he phones again and that's that.'

Penny tried to visualize her father as a criminal. If it was hard for her to see him acting outside the law, how much harder it must be for Nick, who hero-worshipped him. Well, at least it had been Nick who had voiced the thought and not her. She would have been yelled at for hours.

As if he had been reading her mind, Nick qualified his suggestion.

'I don't think it's true, of course. But how can we know?'

Graham Hodge had waited until it was dark, with the vague thought that darkness was an ally. He was in a quiet Edwardian suburb of London and his legs ached from walking the hard pavements and standing, watching.

Looking across the street at the trim privet hedge and the rivered glass door of number sixty-two, he shivered. It had grown appreciably cooler since dusk and his business suit was of a lightweight material. But it was grey. He had an unreasonable faith in the grey colour of the suit. It seemed. . .suitable.

The door of number sixty-two opened and Graham stepped sideways to take cover behind a tree. Since the tree was a slender staked sapling, it was the ludicrous action of a cartoon character rather than of a desperate, three-dimensional man.

The elderly householder did not notice him. Wearing a pink paper party hat, he was talking to his elephantine Persian cat.

'Out you go now. Out you go, sweetie.'

The cat waddled sullenly out of the house, its tail upright and twitching at the tip. The old man lurched a little as he re-entered the house and Graham had the hope that he might have over-indulged. But it could have been old age. It was the age of the occupants that had attracted Graham to this house in the first place.

The door shut again and Graham made up his mind. He crossed the street to the house, where he was accosted by the cat, which seemed to believe he would be able to get it back into the house.

Graham said, 'Go away.' The cat stayed at his feet, at the door. He rang the bell and there was a plinkle of chimes. Through the rivered glass of the door he saw the old man coming back down the hall. The old man opened the door a little way and the cat squirmed in between them.

'Hello? Good evening?'

Graham's mouth was very dry. 'Um — Happy Christmas.'

'Yes?'

'Gas Board,' said Graham, more loudly than he had intended.

'Yes?'

The door wasn't open very far. Graham brought out his credit card folder and let the old man have a glimpse of a defunct store card. 'Regional Manager,' he croaked.

'Yes?'

It was not easy at all. 'We're short-staffed over the Christmas period, so I came myself.' He hurried on before the old man could say 'yes' again. 'We're trying to trace a leak. There's a pipe junction very close to your house, as you may know.'

'Yes?'

You couldn't tell what the old man was thinking. 'So could I come in?'

'Oh. Yes. I suppose you better.'

He allowed Graham to go past him into the house and shut the door. 'What do you want? The kitchen?'

41

'Oh — yes — a quick look.'

They went down the hall into the kitchen. It was evidently the heart of the house, for it doubled as a parlour. A very small old lady was watching a variety show on television, sitting in a deep, broken-springed sofa.

'What is it?' she asked.

There were the remnants of a roast chicken on the kitchen table, Graham noticed. He imagined they were poor.

The old lady tried to get up.

'Gas Board,' said the old man.

'Oh yes?' said his wife.

'A leak, he says.'

'Oh.' She was still trying to get up.

'Stay where you are,' Graham blurted out. He had the feeling he sounded like a gangster. 'I'll — I'll just take a reading.'

Now he took out his pocket electronic organizer. He hoped it looked extremely complicated and high-tech as he pressed a few buttons quickly. His hands were trembling.

'Yes...there's something... You're not on red, though, so there's no danger. Could I take a look upstairs? Gas rises on the warm air of course.'

'Upstairs?' said the old man.

Graham started to leave the room. 'Yes, that's right. I won't be a moment. No — don't let me disturb you. You carry on with your programme.'

Feeling foolish and afraid in equal measure, he walked to the foot of the stairs with his eyes fixed on the display screen of the organizer.

As he went up the stairs he looked down. The old man had not followed him.

Graham walked swiftly to the front bedroom. If there was anything of value in the house, here was the place for it, he felt.

He opened the door into a room full of mementoes of two old people who had spent their lives together. Switching on the light, he saw that every flat surface was a repository for framed photographs. He looked closely at the nearest of these, on the heavy chest of drawers by the door, and saw a family group in black and white, on a beach. The photograph was blurred so that the impression it gave was of smiles and eyes wrinkled up against the sun. A mother, a father, three young children, a dog and a ruined sandcastle. Underneath was written, 'Swanage, 1955'.

Graham could not step further into this very personal place. He had come here to steal from the defenceless. It was the worst action he had ever contemplated in his life. It was unthinkable. He was the lowest form of life imaginable. He would not do it.

He would.

He had to.

'Under the bed,' he whispered viciously. He discovered that to feel thoroughly spiteful was an antidote against self-loathing. He would take one quick look under the bed and then try the dressing-table. There would be something here and he prayed it would be cash.

He lowered himself on to the threadbare carpet. It was dusty and fluffy under the bed and there was nothing there. Lying on the floor he heard a voice, from the room below. His mind worked at its fastest. They used the kitchen as their sitting-room. The front room would be a formal reception room, used once in a blue moon, if at all. But perhaps they had the phone there...

Dust filtered into the back of his throat and he gagged as he rolled out from under the bed. He tiptoed to the top of the stairs, taking huge, delicate *Struwwelpeter* strides.

He heard the old man. 'Oh yes — he's still here. Yes, from the Gas Board he said. Will you? I see. Yes. He didn't look quite right to me. What?'

He was listening to the telephone as Graham abandoned silence and hurtled down the stairs. He twisted his ankle on the last step and clutched at the bannister to get his balance.

The old man came out of the front room and Graham

was face to face with him as he sagged against the bannister. The old man was slack-faced with apprehension.

Graham said, 'It's all right.' He had to cough because of the dust in his throat. 'Nothing to worry about.' He limped to the front door and flung it open. 'There's no gas,' he shouted stupidly, 'it's fine!'

He slammed the door shut and then regretted the noise it made in the quiet street. He mustn't make himself conspicuous. He walked away as fast as he could, with a dread that the old man would open the door and start shouting accusations. None came.

He was sweating. He was as worthless as the dust in his throat.

'At last!' Nick said immediately.

The phone was ringing again, exploding into the boredom of a long evening in front of the television, where everything was glitter and good feeling.

As before, Nick was first to the phone. This time Penny followed him into the study.

'Hi!' he said warmly into the phone, looking at Penny with a hint of triumph.

His expression changed.

'Oh yes — hi.' His hand covered the mouthpiece. 'It's Mum.'

'I'll talk to her,' Penny said and held out her hand for the phone.

Nick said swiftly, 'No,' and swivelled away from her. 'Happy Christmas to you too, Mum.' He listened. 'Yeah — it's been great... No — not much — but it's been fun. You know — all being together.'

He looked at Penny again, who had come round in front of him. 'Yes... So how was yours? Yeah, I bet! Penny? Yes, she's right here.' He handed the phone to his sister, at the same time shaking his head with great emphasis and staring into her eyes.

44

Penny took the phone. 'Hello, Mummy.'

At the moment her mother spoke she was filled with a sense of relief and reassurance at the sound of the familiar tones.

'Hello, darling. Happy Christmas!'

'Happy Christmas,' Penny repeated.

'You've had a quiet day, I hear.'

'Yes.'

Nick came closer, to listen in.

'It's been wonderful here,' came their mother's voice. 'I'm sorry I didn't ring before. One forgets you're a few hours ahead of us here.'

'Yes, that's right.' With a sensation of horror Penny realized she didn't know what to do.

'Could you speak up, darling?'

Penny raised her voice. 'Sorry. Is that better?'

'Yes. Much. Is your father there?'

She felt Nick's hand grasp her arm just above the elbow.

'No — um — that is...'

'Sorry, I can't hear you.'

'Sorry.' She raised her voice again and said clearly, 'He's got a headache. He went to bed early.' Nick's grip relaxed.

'Oh dear. I'm sorry. Tired him out, have you?'

'Mmn. How's Tony?'

'He's very well and happy. We both are. And you are too?'

'Mmn.'

'That's marvellous. Darling — I've got to go down for drinks now. So I just want to say I love you and I miss you and I'll see you soon.'

'Me too,' said Penny foolishly.

'And Happy Christmas.'

'Yes. Happy Christmas. Lots of love.'

'And give Nick a big kiss from me.'

'Yes.'

'Bye, darling.'

'Bye.'

There was that moment's hesitation before they each decided to hang up.

Now Nick let go of her arm fully. 'Thanks.'

'That's OK.' She felt profoundly depressed.

'It was the right thing to do,' Nick said earnestly. 'Dad'll be back soon. He's fine — you don't have to worry.'

CHAPTER 4

ON BOXING Day morning both Penny and Nick stayed in bed until well after it had grown light. Already there was creeping into them the lassitude of prisoners; a feeling that effort of any kind was pointless.

When Penny finally dragged herself out of bed and went to the bathroom she was shocked by her own appearance in the mirror. Her face was the colour of uncooked pastry and there were violet smears of fatigue under her eyes.

'This is ridiculous,' she said aloud.

She had a shower, acting out a scene where someone wakes themselves up under a torrent of freezing water, though for 'freezing' she cautiously substituted 'lukewarm'.

Then she dressed and went down the stairs briskly; fully alert and ready for action. She had no idea as to what action she could take, but some action there must be.

The first thing that caught her eye in the kitchen was the telephone. The telephone... 'Our only link with the outside world,' as she put it to herself. Nick was not here to distract her now and it was morning, and in that fresh and rational time she saw that there was really only one action she could take; and, really, only one person she could call ... One person she *should* call.

In a state of guilty excitement, she ran back upstairs to get her diary. She couldn't help it if it upset Nick, there was simply no other course open to them. She had even written down the international dialling code. Good. It was all so simple.

When she was in the kitchen again, she held the diary open with one hand while the other hovered over the phone as she inwardly composed an opening line. 'Mummy,

47

it's me again. We're all right here — nothing to worry about — but we don't know where Daddy is.' That would do, wouldn't it? She picked up the telephone.

The line was dead. Not a sound of any kind; a truly lifeless silence.

Her chance was gone. But why? Some sort of electrical fault? She looked around, thinking. No — the electricity supply and the telephone line were two separate things, weren't they. . . She looked out of the window and dropped the phone. There was someone in the back garden. She had caught a glimpse of movement behind the garden shed.

And the telephone didn't work. . . With an instinct for self-preservation she ducked below the level of the window and ran, crouched, to the hall door.

Upstairs Nick was asleep, totally covered by his duvet. Penny shook the whole soft pile.

'Get up, Nick. There's someone in the garden.'

'Mmn?'

'In the back garden. There's someone there and the phone's not working.'

'Someone in the garden?'

'Yes.'

He got out of bed and blundered to the window, which overlooked the back garden. They saw that the shed door was open and there was movement in the gloom inside.

'Eric,' Nick said.

'Who?'

'The gardener bloke. I told you — remember?'

'Oh. Eric. . . On Boxing Day?'

'He's a law unto himself, Eric.'

While Nick got dressed Penny stood outside the room and told him about the phone.

'Going to call Mum, were you? Serves you right.' He was still sleepy.

'For a bit I thought someone had cut the wires.'

'More likely we've been cut off because Dad didn't pay the bills.'

48

'Well, I said it might happen.' But it wasn't an 'I told you so' that had any savour for her.

'If they did cut us off, they waited till after Christmas, anyway.'

'Only just.'

'You had your chance,' he said. 'Yesterday. Didn't you?'

Eric Hope was short and square, like the stump of a tree. It was as if a much larger man had been confined in a metal box during his formative years and had come out compacted. He was solid; sort of dense, thought Penny, as he emerged from the shed, wiping his hands on a rag. He wore brown corduroy trousers, a Guernsey pullover and heavy brown shoes. She put his age at about fifty.

'Hello, Nick,' said Eric, breaking his face in half with a hugely wide grin.

'Hi, Eric. What're you up to?'

'Oiling the mower, Nick,' said Eric. 'You have to keep an eye on mechanical things.'

He said it as though it was a quote — an old country saying, perhaps. Penny began to think he might be dense in other than physical ways.

He asked, 'Did you have a nice Christmas?'

Again, 'nice Christmas' was run together as if it came swaddled in quotation marks.

'Not bad,' said Nick.

'I thought I'd do some weeding. Maybe a bit of cutting-back,' Eric continued in his colourless tones. His accent was a strange amalgam of Cambridgeshire and something more urban. Penny could see now why Nick might have thought it a funny notion that they should seek his help.

'You don't have to do anything for weeks, Eric,' Nick said patiently.

Eric grinned again, glowing with joy at his own shrewdness. 'Ah, but it saves time later!'

He stood smiling at them. 'And this is your sister.'

'Yes — this is Penny,' Nick said shortly.

'And you had a nice-Christmas, Penny? Good presents?' Bath salts. 'Not bad, thanks.'

Another quotation rolled out of Eric. 'Christmas is for kiddies.' Another smile.

Kiddies? Penny's mouth started to twitch. Seeing this, Eric broadened his own smile in ready response.

'So where's your Dad?'

Perhaps they were close friends or perhaps Nick liked to provoke Eric, for he answered at once, carelessly. 'He's away again, Eric.'

The effect was magnificent. Eric's mouth turned downwards in an exact reverse of his smile. 'I don't believe it! At Christmas?'

'Well, you know Dad.'

'Christmas is a family time.' Eric shook his head. 'It's not right, Nick.'

'Yeah, well.' Nick raised a hand. 'See you, Eric.'

'Yes. All right, then. Goodbye, Penny. It was nice to meet you.'

Eric held out his hand with a tentative smile. Penny solemnly shook hands with him. His palm was coarse and hard like rusted iron and he gripped very gently.

'Goodbye, Eric.' Already she felt almost protective towards him. Glancing at Nick, who was waiting tolerantly, she had the certain instinct that this man was her brother's only friend.

'I'll be here in the garden this morning, if you want me,' said Eric, as if they didn't know.

'It's too early for pruning. He's a hopeless gardener,' said Nick, in the kitchen.

With great daring, as she thought, Penny had made them both a cup of filter coffee. She was forbidden this adult drink at home and had come to the realization that the smell of ground coffee promised more than it delivered. She added yet another spoonful of sugar and stirred. 'Is he loopy or something?'

'He's been in a funny farm. Now he's in the Care in the Community Programme. Not that anyone does any caring. Except me. I like Eric.'

Penny thought, because you feel superior to him, that's why. She said aloud, 'He's very conscientious, anyway.'

'Oh yes. Probably because he's simple. He's got very strict ideas about right and wrong, too. You can't half shock him sometimes.' He grinned and then gave a kind of sneer of irritation. 'This is terrible.'

'Sorry. I didn't know how much to put in.'

'Not the coffee. Us. Sitting around here. We've got to *do* something. I mean it, Penny.'

'Oh, do stop. What can we do? Get to a phone? Call Mummy? Call Granny?'

His irritation mounted. 'No. *Do* something, not talk.'

'We could go for a walk, I suppose.'

'Oh, shut up. You don't know what it's like for me. One minute you know exactly where you are and the next... It's all crazy.' He burst out, 'It's not fair!'

'What? Not having any money suddenly?'

'You shut up. Not knowing. That's what's not fair.'

He stood up and walked to the phone. He lifted it from the receiver and listened. Obviously the line was still dead, for all at once he ran backwards and ripped the flex from the receiver. Then he threw the phone across the room. It hit the pinewood dresser with a crack.

'I don't see how that helps,' said Penny. 'You could have broken something.'

'I'd like to break something.' Nick made fists of his hands. 'He doesn't pay the bills. He runs off... I'm going to see Mr Sheridan.' He began to walk out of the room. Penny sprang to her feet. She beat Nick to the hall door and stood there in his way.

'Wait a minute. You can't leave me here.'

51

'Why not?'

'Anyway — I don't see how it could help. Mr Sheridan's the man who sacked him, isn't he? He can't help — he sacked him.'

'Why? That's what I want to know.' He repeated desperately, 'I want to know! And they were friends and everything. And perhaps Mr Sheridan knows what he's been doing since.'

'He might... But I wouldn't go, if I was you.'

'Well, you're not.'

'You should ring first. It's Boxing Day. He might not want to see you.'

'Who cares what he wants? He fired my father. Anyway, I'm glad now I can't call him. It'd be better just to turn up.'

'I don't think it would, you know...'

'Well, I'm going anyway and you can't stop me. I've had enough of it here.'

'Then I'm coming too,' Penny said. 'If you're really going.' She might have added, 'Because it's not right to leave me alone here', but that was not her only reason for tagging along. She could see only too clearly that an interview with Mr Sheridan could be very painful for Nick.

They walked into the village in silence. The lack of talk stemmed from Nick, who wore a glowering expression. In an effort to look older and more responsible he had put on his father's soft leather jacket and a pair of his trousers. The effect was of a spoilt rich boy, Penny thought.

There was a restricted service today and the bus they waited for was late, too. A few families walked about the village aimlessly, with a view to retrieving an appetite for rich food.

Once a boy on a bike nodded to Nick and he nodded back.

'Who was that?' Penny asked timidly.

'I don't know. Just someone who lives here.'

It had broken their silence.

'You haven't even told me where we're going.'

'Cambridge. Well—just outside. The bus goes all the way. When it comes.'

When it came it was a single-decker carrying few passengers, with a driver who was cheerful and unapologetic about his late arrival at the stop. They slid into seats near the back.

'You just have to be able to drive in the country these days,' said Nick. He was less sullen now they were on their way.

'You're too young to drive, anyway.'

'I was learning. Dad let me have a go every now and then. He's terrific like that.'

'What—on the roads?'

'Sure,' Nick said nonchalantly. 'You don't know Dad at all. He's not like he was with us. He's really great.' He looked out of the window. 'He used to be.'

'I suppose he sold the car because he needed the money.'

Silence fell on them again as the level countryside streamed by.

'Haven't we come too far? It's been all houses for ages.'

'Next stop. The villages all got joined up round here.'

'But you do know where we're going?'

'I've been there lots of times. Well—a couple. He gives a summer garden party for the firm. We didn't go this year. Dad said he couldn't be bothered...'

A minute or so later, the bus jolted to a stop. They stepped down. The driver said, 'Take care now.' Perhaps he knew something they didn't.

Nick led the way down a wide street of modern houses, where pavements ran through the close-cropped grass verges. At the end was the brick gateway to a private estate. A sign said 'No Thoroughfare'.

'This is it?' said Penny. She was incredibly nervous.

'This is it.' He marched on through the gates. When

they had passed four or five large mock-Georgian houses he stopped. The next house looked attractive to Penny. Wisteria climbed its walls, ageing and softening the hard brick lines; the front lawn was less well-tended than those of the neighbouring houses; it seemed approachable.

But Nick had come to a standstill. 'Perhaps they're not in.'

Penny said nothing. She thought she could hear music coming from somewhere in the house. A disco sound. They were in, all right. Nick must be as nervous as she was.

'We don't have to go on with this,' she said reasonably.

'Yes, we do.' Nick opened the gate and walked up the path. Penny wished she hadn't spoken. Somehow she had goaded him on. Oh well. She caught up with him at the door, which had a festive wreath attached to the lion's-head knocker. There was a brass bell-push, too. Nick wiped a sweating palm on his trousers and pressed the bell.

After a short pause thunderous footsteps cascaded down the stairs. Giggles. The door was opened by a very pretty teenage girl in jeans and a baggy blue angora sweater. She had ash blonde hair. Another ash blonde head was at her shoulder; her younger sister, equally pretty.

The taller blonde was disappointed. 'Oh. Hello.'

'Edward's not coming — I said he wouldn't,' her sister said.

'What do you want?' said the older girl. 'Do I know you?'

'Well...um...I'm Nick,' said Nick. 'We have met, actually.'

'Oh yes,' the girl said with the serene indifference of the accepted beauty. 'Yes, that's right. Your father's Graham Thingy, isn't he.'

'Mmn.'

'You haven't said what you want, yet,' said the other blonde.

Penny said, 'Is your father in?'

Nick added quickly, 'I want to see him.'

'*I* don't,' the younger one giggled. 'He's got a dreadful hangover today.'

'Well, I do,' said Nick definitely. 'I do want to see him.'

'Oh come in,' said the older girl.

Her sister ran away up the broad stairway. 'Bye,' she called gaily.

'You can wait in here.' They went into the drawing-room, while the girl went off down the corridor.

The drawing-room was delightfully chaotic. The spirit of a Christmas enjoyed to the full could be seen not only in the broad spruce tree in the window, heavy with decoration, but in the torn swathes of wrapping paper of all colours and designs; the crumbs of food on the elegant Chinese carpet, and the great bowl of shattered nuts on a low, polished table which was sticky from the rims of countless glasses.

Under the Christmas tree there were still some unopened presents, no doubt for friends and relations who would be visiting later. Or sooner — or now... It was a disaster coming here, Penny thought. And she thought, too, 'These kids have got it made, and they don't know it.' She could not feel resentful, however. They had seemed quite charming to her. It would probably be nice to be a part of this family.

Nick mumbled, 'I don't know what to say to him.'

'Well, we're here now. We'll have to make the best of it.' Another of her mother's phrases.

'Thanks a lot.'

The blonde came back looking flushed and severely embarrassed without losing one fraction of her appeal. Probably she could cry and still look attractive, thought Penny, who in that instant felt like crying herself.

'I shouldn't have let you in, I don't think. I got a lecture. Still — you can see him. If you really want to.'

'Thanks a lot,' said Nick, with no sarcasm this time.

'Come on, then.'

She led the way down the hall. Upstairs a woman's voice called, 'If you get the receipt from her you can exchange it.'

A younger voice called back, 'She won't have kept it.'

'Well. . .it's not *that* bad, is it?'

'Yes! Hopeless!'

The girl left them by an open door opposite the kitchen, from which there came aromas of something curried.

'There you go.' The beauty allowed them a small smile from her stock of gracious expressions and swung away back down the hall with every pale, perfect hair on her head bouncing in unison.

Unlike his erstwhile employee, Mr Sheridan had more of a library than a study. There were fitted bookshelves filled with glossy hardback books, and weighty red leather furniture was scattered about. The impression of being in a gentlemen's club was unpleasantly enhanced by the smell of stale cigar smoke. The velvet curtains were half-shut. It was oppressive; not at all cosy.

Mr Sheridan could have been dressed for a game of golf as he lay on the Chesterfield sofa in his yellow shirt and check trousers. He looked both sleepy and thoroughly fed up; though perhaps that was his usual expression. He was big in a well-fed sort of way and his heavy-lidded eyes gave him a vaguely patrician look.

'Nick. . .' he said heavily.

'Yes.'

'Where's your father?' It was, of course, the key question, but fortunately he went on without seeing how taken aback his guests were. 'Not with you?'

'No.'

'That your sister?'

'Yes.'

Mr Sheridan sat up and put his feet on the floor and his head in his hands.

'This is Christmas, Nick,' he sighed.

'I know.'

'What am I supposed to say to you? Or have you come here to say something to me?'

'I don't know,' Nick said weakly.

Mr Sheridan looked up. 'Did he send you?'

'No. I...we came because I wanted to know...'

Suddenly Mr Sheridan was incisive. 'Know what? Come on—get on with it.'

'Why did you sack him?' Nick said loudly.

He might not have been feeling well, but his confidence was unimpaired.

'Ah. I see... Because I felt I should. So I did. I liked your father—you know that. But I'm responsible to and for a lot of people. And I have to keep my business competitive.' He waited a second. 'Is that it?'

'No. You didn't have to get rid of him. He was good at his job, I know he was.'

Now Mr Sheridan got up. 'If he sent you here I'm going to be very angry. He got rid of himself, Nick. There was nothing I could do about it.'

'He said you were friends.'

The man swore and said, 'This is really too bad—it really isn't on! You shouldn't be here. I don't know what Daisy was thinking of.' He put his hands in his pockets and said forcefully, 'Your father was fired because he had his hand in the till.' Nick visibly flinched. 'He was appropriating money that was not his. Now that's the truth and I'm sorry about it and I'm not surprised he couldn't find it in him to tell you himself. Now I think you should go.'

Nick held his ground. 'Does that mean he couldn't get another job?'

'How old are you?' Mr Sheridan abruptly asked Penny.

When she shrugged, unable to speak, he said, 'I don't know why I should let you two do this to me. What do you think I *am*?' He turned back to Nick. 'No, if you're asking, I did not let it be known that your dad was dishonest. I should have but I didn't.' He was restless with bad humour. 'It's not my fault if he didn't get another job. Or has he got one now?'

Nick and Penny absorbed the information in these remarks.

'I'm sorry I came,' Nick said in an emotional whisper.

It could almost have been taken for an apology, and it made Mr Sheridan angrier still, apparently.

'*You're* sorry? You come here and tell me I'm some sort of Scrooge or something, and —'

'We didn't.' Penny's voice returned to her. 'We wanted to know.'

Mr Sheridan sat down again. 'OK. OK... So now you know. You'd better go now. I'd drive you, but...' but he didn't want to. 'I won't tell him you came. OK? You shouldn't have, anyway.' His eyelids started to close of their own accord, it seemed, and he lay back on the sofa. 'You shouldn't have come.'

'No,' Penny said. 'I know.'

The house itself, suffused with seasonal cheer, remained welcoming as they passed down the hall to the front door and the quiet streets beyond.

Outside it wasn't cold, but it might just as well have been.

They walked past the bus stop they had alighted at and went onwards for several hundred yards to the next. Neither wanted to linger near the estate.

It was an age-long wait for the bus. Penny said at last, 'I suppose we should have known it would be something like that.'

Nick only said, 'I'm thinking,' though in all probability it was feelings he was trying to deal with, not thoughts.

The single-decker bus roared towards them and lurched to a stop with hissing noises of brakes and automatic doors. The doors shut behind them with that jerky, robotic motion and they paid their fares and the bus jolted off with a grinding of gears.

It was two o'clock by now and they were the only people on board. This driver was taciturn and in a mysterious hurry. The long vehicle careered down the roads as if it were a fire engine on the way to a conflagration. There was a strange abandonment in this rapid travel and they began to talk.

'I don't care what he thinks about Daddy,' Penny said.

'He wasn't a very nice man. Perhaps you have to be a bit of a horror to be successful in business.'

Nick felt momentarily very old. 'No,' he said wearily, 'he's not so bad. What could we expect him to say? We put him on the spot.'

'Good,' Penny said with emphasis. 'And at least we did something. That's what you wanted, wasn't it.'

Her brother flared up at this. 'But we didn't — we didn't do anything. We stood about and listened, but we didn't do anything.'

'What are you saying?'

Nick wasn't sure. He was feeling ineffectual, and it brought to mind a thousand other occasions on which he had felt inadequate. A thousand humiliations. At school; at sports. Never the courage to do anything daring. He was someone who made up the numbers and that was all. In any confrontation where there was a threat of physical violence, he backed down. He was a coward who could never summon up the will to act as he wanted to act. He was even cowardly at lessons. When questioned directly by a master, answers he knew perfectly well flew out of his head. One boy had started a one-man campaign to get him nicknamed 'The Wimp'. He would have liked to smash the boy into bits, but of course he hadn't, and fortunately nobody was interested enough in him to honour him with a nickname.

He was timorous and uninteresting and only with his father did he feel that he was in any way special and important.

'We'll go and find him,' he said.

'What? You're joking!'

'No. If he's not at home now, well, we've got a London address for him. He might be in trouble — we know he might. Well, we'll go to London and. . .make enquiries,' he finished self-consciously.

'No, we can't do that. We've done enough.'

'We haven't done *anything*!' It was a howl of frustration.

59

'He said—just wait. *You* said...you said he'd be back.'

'He's in trouble and I want to find him and I'll go by myself if I have to.'

'That's not fair! You know I wouldn't stay there by myself!'

'Well, there you are, then.' He smiled complacently. 'Have you got any money? Dad's left me a bit short recently.'

An intense discussion developed, kept at a level beneath the driver's hearing. Given the bone-shaking nature of the bus ride, this permitted raised voices. Penny argued the case for responsibility and common sense and Nick clung to the principle that if he was allowed to do exactly as he wanted, the world would be a better place.

There was no moving him. Physically shaken and emotionally stirred, they stepped down from the bus in the village.

By now Penny was concentrating on damage-limitation. '*If* we go, we've got to tell someone what we're doing. We can't just disappear, like Daddy.' That was a telling one, she thought.

'*When* we go, we'll leave a note at the cottage.'

'No. It's not good enough. We've got to have someone who knows where we are all along.'

At the end of the long, straight, deserted High Street, someone was bicycling towards them.

A square, ponderous figure who cycled slowly, keeping well into the kerb.

'Eric,' Nick said. 'We'll tell Eric.'

CHAPTER 5

FOR REASONS known only to himself, or for no reason at all, Eric cycled by them with no more than a distant smile.

Nick and Penny did not want to tell him at once, anyway. The first thing to do was to get back to the cottage to see if Graham had come back in their absence. Nick now rather hoped he hadn't, while Penny fervently hoped he had.

He hadn't.

They were tired and could not face an immediate return to the village and Eric, so they re-opened their argument for half an hour and then set off again for the village more tired than ever.

'He lives alone,' Nick said as they trudged along. 'His mother died last year.'

Penny didn't think of most middle-aged men as having mothers, but with Eric it seemed natural enough.

'They didn't get on,' Nick added. 'I think he was glad.'

'Why? Why didn't they get on?'

'I don't know. Probably she was ashamed of him.'

And this is the person we're going to confide in, thought Penny: a dimbo-brain. But she hadn't the energy for any more quarrelling.

Eric's house was on the other side of the village in a road going nowhere, superseded by a more major thoroughfare which swept round to the new estate. The house was in a tight row of glazed-brick dwellings with metal surrounds to their windows. 'Dwellings' would have been the description when they were first advertised; now, less aptly, they would be sold as 'cottages'.

Eric's bicycle was chained to the party fence to the next house, so that the thin garden path was almost impassable.

Nick knocked on the octagon of dimpled glass above the letter box. They waited and Eric's big head swam into view in the octagon, as he tried to make out the identity of his callers. After a few moments he opened the door.

'Hello!' The big smile, but anxiety too. 'Hello, Nick.' To Penny: 'I'm sorry — I've forgotten your name.'

'Penny.'

'That's it. Penny.'

'Can we come in, Eric?' Nick asked.

'Why?'

'We want to see you.'

'We saw each other just now,' Eric said reasonably.

'Well, we've been thinking since then.'

'Your dad's away, isn't he... Has he come back?'

'That's what we've been thinking about.'

'Or is he still away?'

'He's still away. We wanted to talk to you.'

'You went off without telling me.'

Perhaps he had been hurt by this, which was why he had bicycled past them without stopping.

'Yes, well...' Nick said.

'And then I saw you in the street.'

'Yes.'

Eric digested this summary of their dealings that day. 'Would you like some tea?'

Penny said, 'Yes, that'd be lovely.'

A dreadful doubt attacked Eric. 'I don't know if I should.'

Nick was short with him. 'Oh, don't be stupid, Eric — we're friends, aren't we?'

'Yes, but...I'm nice and everything, but you can't go around inviting kiddies to tea. Some people have got into trouble with that.'

'This is special, Eric. And we are friends.'

'I could say you came to bring back something I left at your home,' Eric deliberated.

'You don't have to say anything. Can we come in now?'

'Um...yes. Come in.'

They squeezed past Eric into the house. Eric took a quick look up and down the street and closed the door. He turned round.

'I haven't Hoovered today,' he said, finding something else to worry about.

'It's Christmas,' Nick said reassuringly.

'It's a Bissel, really,' said Eric obliquely.

Penny thought the hall carpet would look awful however clean it was. Once crimson, it had faded to magenta and the huge yellow flowers on it were turning brown. It ran onwards up the steep flight of stairs into the darkness at the top.

'We'll have tea in the kitchen,' Eric said cheerfully, feeling more relaxed. 'Three spoonfuls and one for the pot.' He was leading the way down the hall and now he stopped and looked back. 'I don't believe in tea-bags,' he said quietly.

They went on to where the carpet gave way to brown linoleum. The kitchen furniture was white laminated assemble-yourself.

'Make yourselves at home!' Eric said.

Penny and Nick sat down at the small table. For some reason it did not seem at all rude to wait idly while Eric busied himself around the room.

'Kettle...' He filled the aluminium kettle and put it on the gas stove. 'Self-igniting,' he said proudly. 'Tea-pot. Tea. Oh — biscuits...'

Penny saw how orderly were the contents of the kitchen cupboards as Eric plucked out a packet of tea and a round tin of biscuits.

'You're very neat,' she said.

'Plates,' he replied, kneeling down to a lower cupboard. 'I'm sorry there's no cake.'

'Oh, that doesn't matter,' Nick said impatiently.

Eric took out three pale blue plates and set them on the table. 'Kiddies like cake... I had some. I had some, but I ate it.' He smiled at how very foolish he had been. 'I can sit down for a minute,' he reminded himself, and did so.

Just as Nick was about to speak he said, 'Waiting for the kettle. Army.'

Penny had been gazing out of the back window, where, despite Eric's interest in gardening, there was only a simple strip of lawn. She realized that Eric was looking at her.

'Sorry?'

'I was in the army,' Eric explained. 'They have everything just-so in the army. You get used to it.'

'Sorry?'

'You wanted to know about my cupboards.'

'I didn't know you were in the army, Eric,' Nick said, slightly affronted. 'You never said.'

'Oh well. It was a long time ago. I was a Young Man.' He might as well have said he was a dog, in those far-off days. 'I jumped out of aeroplanes and — oh — everything. We did everything. I sustained an injury, unfortunately, which stopped it. That's when my troubles started.'

'What. . .you fell on your head or something?' Nick joked crudely.

Eric nodded agreement. 'It was something like that. They said. . .' He paused for effect and somehow Penny knew the exact phrase he would use next. 'They said I was lucky-to-be-alive.' Then, in case they were on tenterhooks about it, he said, 'I'll warm the tea-pot in a minute. I use boiling.'

'And that's where you got all neat,' Penny prompted him. 'In the army.' Nick gave her a dirty look.

'Yes, that's where. Hospitals and. . .and places like that are neat too, but you don't do so much for yourself. In the camp you look after yourself and they like you to keep things in their proper place, in case anybody sees.'

'In the army camp — yes.'

'In the holiday camp,' Eric said.

'What?'

Nick shifted in his chair. 'He worked in a holiday camp. I know all about that.'

'Have a biscuit,' Eric said. 'They're not very nice.' He offered the tin to Penny. 'I got too many.'

They were all shapes, sugar-dusted, some with red jellified centres. Penny knew what Eric meant when she bit into one and it quickly turned into soggy flour in her mouth.

'I know what you mean — but they're not too bad.'

'Stale,' said Eric sadly. 'At the camp, you wouldn't believe the waste. Food chucked away ... Tons of it.'

'The holiday camp?'

'Nothing was too good for our campers. I was so lucky to get that job.'

Nick said quickly, 'The reason we're here, Eric —'

' "Fun at the Pool," ' Eric reminisced.

'Dad's been away for —'

' "Under Twelves' Treasure Hunt. A Prize for every Contestant." Can you believe that? "Show us your legs, Missus!" ' He laughed warmly.

'Oh come on, Eric — you were only there two years.' Nick tried everything to shift Eric from his pet subject.

Eric got up and went to the stove. 'Two seasons. "Seasons", they call them.' He stood waiting for the kettle to boil. 'They took me on as a lifeguard at the pool. You wouldn't believe how good that was. You saw ...' He searched for a way of communicating to Penny the nature of this golden era. 'Kiddies having fun,' he said finally. 'The pool was best. But the next season I was doing all sorts of things — night work, too. Cleaning. I wasn't at the pool any more. But I saw all the shows. You could look at the faces of the mums and dads and they were smiling. . . Nobody got bored. We didn't let them!'

At last the kettle boiled and Eric's attention focused on his duties as host.

Warm the pot. Measure in the tea. Boiling water poured in. Milk to be put on the table. Mugs. Oh, and a strainer to catch the leaves coming out of the spout. Tea spoons. Sugar ...

'Sugar? Kiddies like sugar, don't they.' He sat down again at the little table, with Penny and Nick. The three of them were very close together. 'Now we wait till the tea's the right colour.'

'Then can we talk now, Eric?' Nick asked with heavy irony.

'Oh yes, of course. Say whatever you like.' He looked at Penny. 'That's what I learnt at the camp. "Kiddies are VIPs here", they used to say. It's true. Kiddies are very important people.'

There was a silence. Nick was waiting to see if Eric's holiday camp information had dried up. Apparently it had.

'Eric. I think we need your help.'

'Help,' Eric said blankly.

'Yes. You see—'

'Tea might be ready.' Eric poured a little tea into his mug. 'Just about.' His anxiety returned. 'Shall I pour the milk in first, or the tea?'

'It doesn't matter.'

Nick was very tense by now.

'I'll do it my way, then. Milk first.'

They waited until the three mugs were filled with milk and tea and, under Eric's approving gaze, they had helped themselves to sugar.

Penny took a sip. 'Lovely.'

'Good.' Eric looked at Nick.

'Terrific.'

'That's good.' Eric drank from his mug. 'No, it's not too bad, is it! I wish you'd tell me why you wanted to see me. It was a surprise.'

Now his chance had come, Nick spoke very rapidly. 'Dad's gone away, Eric. I know he does that every now and then, but it's Christmas and there's something wrong. He...he's lost his job. He didn't tell me. Now he's taken off and we want to know where he is. We know there's a place in London where he might be, but we can't get in touch. He rang up and he sounded ...'

66

Penny took over. 'He sounded so funny. Something's really wrong.'

'He could even be in trouble with the police,' Nick said. 'That's what makes it all...'

'Police?' It wasn't a word Eric liked.

'Well, we don't know how he gets his money,' Penny said painfully. 'And he seemed so strange. Upset.'

'We just don't know what's going on. We want to know a bit more before — well, before we do anything.'

'What about your mum?' Eric said. He was acutely uneasy, and Penny was not surprised.

She said, 'She's abroad.' There was absolutely no need to mention honeymoons. 'We can't think of anyone we can talk to about it. Except the police, and we don't want to do that.'

'No,' Eric agreed vigorously, 'no.'

'We've been through it all over and over, Eric,' said Nick, 'and the best thing for us to do is to go and have a quick look for him.'

'In London,' Penny said. She half hoped Eric would dismiss the idea as mad.

What Eric said, after a second, was, 'Police... Well — do you know — he hasn't paid me for weeks, your dad...' He added politely, 'Not that I'm in a hurry. Police...' The word seemed to fascinate him into immobility, like a torch shone on a wild animal or bird.

'You don't understand,' Nick said. 'All we need is that someone — it could be anyone and we've picked you — knows what we're doing in case anyone else wants to know or needs to know. Do you get it?'

'No.'

'Someone's got to know where we've gone.'

'London.'

'Yes.'

Eric got up.

'You can't go to London!'

'We've got to.'

'No! You can't have kiddies wandering around London! It's not a very nice place!'

'Penny lives there. We both know it quite well, actually,' Nick said pompously.

'No, no — oh no. What if your father comes back and I have to talk to him!' Eric put the lid on the biscuit tin, distractedly, and took the tin to the cupboard.

'We wouldn't be there long.'

'You can't do it, Nick! No!'

'Well, we're going to and you know about it now, so we've done what we came for, when you think about it.'

Eric turned to him. 'That's not fair.'

'Sorry,' said Nick triumphantly.

'I can't let you do it, Nick. I'm grown up.'

'Sorry...'

'You can't have kiddies wandering around without someone else — it's not right.'

'We're going. Tomorrow morning.'

Eric came back to the table, still clutching the biscuit tin. He was very distressed. 'I'll come with you,' he said.

Oh no, Penny thought.

'Thinking about it, it's brilliant.'

They were on the sofa in the sitting-room, where Penny had insisted on turning on every available light. She had not enjoyed their walk home in the dark.

'It's crazy,' she said.

'No — look — if we have to ask questions or anything — if we have to talk to anyone — well, we've got an adult with us. We could say he was our uncle, or something.'

'You can tell him that. I'm not going to.'

'He'll go along with it. He doesn't mind doing what you tell him to do.'

' "Ask" him to.'

'All right — ask him to. He doesn't mind.'

Not only had Nick welcomed the jobbing gardener's participation, Eric himself had been tiresomely insistent. He had discovered a phrase which said it all and repeated it endlessly. 'Kiddies should not be left unattended.' Perhaps it was another distorted relic of the great days at the holiday camp. Penny had despaired. She told herself that any other adult would have tried to dissuade Nick, rather than taking his senseless plan as a starting point for discussion.

'I still think it's worse than before,' she now said.

'Nah. He's not much use, but it'll be kind of good to have him around.'

'Comforting?'

'If you like.' He got up, business-like. 'We'd better have a proper look at the money situation. We'll bring it down here, OK?'

Penny was reluctant, but found it impossible to argue about such a minor detail, though she knew intuitively that her doubts about the expedition were quite immaterial if her every action committed her further.

Laid out on the sitting-room floor, the money clearly did not amount to riches. Nick had a lot of coins in his pile and only one note.

'That's twelve pounds and sixty pence. What have you got?'

'Eight pounds of my own and ten Mummy gave me for emergencies.'

'Well, this is an emergency, isn't it? I hope Eric pays for himself. I would normally have more, but Dad hasn't come through with the allowance recently.'

They thought about that for a moment and then Penny said, ' "Allowance", is it? I get pocket money.'

'Well, we've got enough, anyway. Who's going to be banker?'

'We'll look after our own,' said Penny, drawing back a stray pound coin into her pile.

'You would say that. You've got more.'

'It's not my fault.' There was a spark of resistance still. 'Anyway, actually we haven't got enough.'

'Sure we have. Two cheap day-returns and a few tube fares. Plenty.'

She couldn't resist showing her superior knowledge. 'You can get a one-day travelcard for everywhere in London.'

'There you are, then. You should be pleased — we can only afford to do one day anyway. So you should be happy.'

In the night, Penny knocked on Nick's door.

'I can't sleep, Nick.'

'Nor can I. Come in, if you like.'

It was cold. She had brought her duvet with her. In the darkness she sat down on the carpet and wrapped the duvet around her.

'Nick. . .'

'Mmn.'

'I just wish he'd come back.'

'Do you think I don't?'

'I don't know. I think you're looking forward to tomorrow.'

'I am, in a way. And in a way I'm not at all. It's funny.'

'Hysterical.'

Her sarcasm kept him quiet for a while and it was she who had to re-open the conversation. 'We're not going to get anything out of this. I know we're not.'

'He might be at his flat. Could easily be.'

'He might not, either.'

'There'll be people to ask. Like I said, with Eric with us, we can ask questions without anyone getting all concerned about us. It's a wonderful piece of luck.'

Again she took the opportunity for sarcasm. 'Wonderful.'

After some minutes of uncomfortable silence they both drifted off to sleep, though in the morning both would claim they had not slept at all.

Graham Hodge woke before daybreak. Like Penny on the floor in her brother's room, he had been cramped and cold. On his arrival, already in the early hours, he had been surprised to find the benches had been removed from both sides of the brick shelter in the little park he had wandered into. But it was at least warmer here than out in the elements and he had been sick of walking the streets.

He stretched, and his back hurt, and the tendons behind his knees. He had been in a crouching position in the angle where the walls met and now he wondered if his legs would straighten, and then, if they would bear his weight.

He turned his head to exercise his neck. At the junction of two footpaths a sodium light shone from a lamppost and by its diffused yellow light he saw he was no longer alone in the shelter. There were two bundles of dark clothes in the corner across from his. Only one face was visible, and silver in the man's beard-stubble caught the light. A hand grasped a nearly-full bottle of cider. Foresight. Breakfast.

Graham lurched painfully to his feet. He couldn't stay here with these vagrants. Under his shoes there were bleached sweet wrappers and empty beer cans. Stepping out of the shelter, he scrunched one the cans. The sleepers did not stir.

He didn't know exactly where he was. Somewhere in North London, that was all he knew. He pulled his jacket tightly about him and limped off, going in no particular direction, but going. His ankle still hurt. His whole body hurt.

He could feel the organizer in his breast pocket, hard against his ribs. It came to him that this was a negotiable asset. It held essential information, true, yet it might fetch a fair sum, and today there would be shops open. He could not try any form of felony again. Unless a cast-iron, consequence-free opportunity presented itself. . .

The bulky feel of the organizer gave him confidence. He began to walk faster, trying to create warmth.

'You look dreadful.'

'It's all I've got. I've got to keep warm,' Penny said defensively.

She had put on jeans and the kind of trainers that make feet look enormous. Her voluminous pink sweater was trying to grow new sweaters by way of the tiny wool balls which clung to it all over, and she carried the old school mac that would put the finishing touch to the ensemble.

'You look like someone who should be taken into care,' said Nick.

'Well, you look like a complete greaseball.'

Once again Nick had dressed from his father's wardrobe, choosing highly-creased pale trousers and a blue jumper with red triangles on it, over which was the leather jacket.

'I want to look respectable — as if we've got some money. We may have to talk to people.'

'So you keep saying.' She managed a dry tone.

'Is everything turned off?'

'I think so.'

'OK. I'll lock up. If we walk slowly we'll be dead on time. Do you have to take that bag?'

'Mummy gave it to me. It's useful.'

'It's awful. What is it — Ethiopian? From a charity shop?'

'Don't start, Nick.'

It was one of those pale, soulless days that are strangely calming, and they saw no one on the way to the village. They walked slowly and yet to Penny the journey had already begun to seem shorter through familiarity.

Nick had brought with him a couple of giveaway train time-tables. He had consulted them so often last night and this morning that he could have known them by heart. Now he stumbled from time to time as he re-read them on the walk.

As they approached Eric's house the gardener came out of his front door. Probably he had been looking out for them through the window. Eric locked the door and looked up and down the street; then he gave Nick and Penny a small wave of his big hand.

'Well,' said Penny, 'if you think *I* look odd...'

In fact, there was nothing very odd about Eric's clothes. It was only that he looked uncomfortable in them. Above his corduroy trousers he had on a check shirt and V-necked jumper, and over that a tweed jacket. It was the jacket that ruled one's impression of him. It was old and a little greasy and it moulded itself to his body like putty, except at the flapping double vent over his bottom. The whole effect was of an unsuccessful farmer.

'Oh well,' said Nick philosophically. 'Good morning, Eric,' he called.

'Hello, Nick. Good morning, um...'

'Penny,' said Penny.

'Yes, that's it. I'm glad you're not late.'

'We won't miss the bus, don't worry,' Nick said.

They waited while Eric carefully shut the garden gate behind him. 'Ready.'

'Off we go, then,' said Nick.

They saw Eric look up and down the road again and smiled at one another. Eric saw them, but it did not matter; he smiled too. Perhaps he was looking forward to the day out.

Christmas was on the wane and the bus to Cambridge picked up and set down passengers at almost every stop.

Eric spoke at a conspiratorial level. 'It's a flat, then, where we're going?'

'Yes,' said Nick.

'In London.'

'Yes.'

'Where?'

'I'm not quite sure. I couldn't find any London street books in the house.' It had been a matter of extreme frustration for Nick.

73

'You've never been there? To this flat?'

'No.'

To Penny, 'But you have, though, um...'

'Penny. No. We only just found out about it. It's South West, but I don't know which side of the river.'

Eric said slowly, 'We don't know where we're going, then...'

'Not exactly,' said Penny, just as Nick said, 'Sort of.'

Eric sat back and took in some deep breaths which he forced out through his nose, noisily. Then he said, 'Oh dear,' quite calmly. 'Oh dear. Oh dear.'

'Do shut up, Eric,' said Nick. 'We're going to buy an *A to Z* in London, first thing we do.'

Eric did not speak again. He looked out of the window and did some more breathing. The volume of air he produced from his nose seem disproportionate to the small amount he breathed in.

'Are you going to do that all the way to Cambridge?' Nick asked.

Eric did do it all the way to Cambridge and the woman in front of them looked round three times in naked disapproval before she gave up. Penny and Nick let Eric's breathing substitute for conversation. The journey seemed long and curiously tiring.

In Cambridge they had to board another bus to get to the station. Eric stopped his breathing trick and took notice of his surroundings.

'It's a nice place to spend a day, Cambridge,' he said hopefully. Neither of his companions rose to this. They were thinking their own thoughts.

At the station, Nick wondered aloud if they should get something to read on the train.

'Better not,' said Penny. 'Think of the money.'

Nick thought of the money and agreed and then asked Eric, brusquely, if he had enough money on him.

'Oh yes,' Eric answered sadly. 'Plenty.' Nick and Penny exchanged glances of relief.

'Day return, Eric,' Nick ordered. 'Ask for a—'

'I know how to do it, thank you,' Eric said, on his dignity. He cheered up while they waited for the train, reassured by the presence of the return ticket he had stowed safely in his jacket pocket.

'Longest platform in England, Cambridge has,' he informed them. 'Or perhaps it used to be. I'm not sure now. I've been a train-spotter in my time.'

Just before the train was due Nick said, 'Get in when it comes,' and raced away down the platform. 'Back in a sec,' he called over his shoulder. They saw him disappear into the station buffet. He was still there when the train arrived. Eric and Penny let others board the train while they waited for him by an open carriage door. He ran back to them with three cans in his hands.

'Just made it! Get in. . .get in! Do you want us to miss it?'

They stepped up into the carriage and walked along it to where they would not have to sit too close to anyone.

The train began to pull out of the station by infinitesimal degrees.

'Lemonade,' said Nick. 'I got one for you too, Eric.'

'Thanks,' said Eric dully. He took the can without looking. He was watching the platform passing by.

Nick gave a can to Penny. 'Had to do it. There isn't a buffet car on this train, so. . . You see, we've got to have a positive attitude! That's how you get things done.'

For the life of her Penny could not see how buying some soft drinks encouraged a positive attitude. Still, if it made Nick happy. . .

The train gathered speed and Eric craned his neck to see the station disappear. Nick and Penny opened their lemonade cans and drank. When he could no longer see any part of the station, Eric started his breathing trick again.

Nick said, 'Eric, if you're going to do that, you can go straight home.'

'It's a thing I learnt. It makes you peaceful.' He breathed out one last time through his nose. 'I couldn't go home and leave you in London. It wouldn't be right.' He leant forward, the can nearly invisible in his hand. 'They said — doctors — they said...' He paused. 'It was just one doctor really. He said I mustn't do anything that made me feel uncomfortable with myself. Do you see?'

'See what?' said Penny.

'I couldn't let you go to London by yourselves. That would make me uncomfortable with myself.'

He sat back again, holding the unopened lemonade can.

The train hurried on.

Eric looked uncomfortable.

CHAPTER 6

OF THE two London stations serving Cambridge, King's Cross has altered least over the years.

Not so very long ago one could buy cheap shirts imported from unidentified countries of origin. The labels simply said, 'Empire-Made'. King's Cross was Empire made. Under its great iron-girdered, hanger-like roofs it was not hard to visualize steam locomotives hissing in and out, drawing first-, second-, and third-class carriages. The station has confidence. 'The Empire is great; its hub, London, is great; you are small.'

To add to this effect, London is one of those places where the volume seems to be turned up. It had not occurred to Penny, a Londoner herself, that her own city could ever appear strange to her; but standing with Eric outside a W.H. Smith's on King's Cross station she felt alien and very alone, just as a foreigner might. Worse than that, she felt herself to be an impoverished foreigner, one that would travel third-class should the means to do so still exist.

Like Moses bearing the Ten Commandments, Nick joined them importantly with a paperback *A to Z*. 'Now we'll know what we're doing.'

It seemed a lot to ask of a street directory.

'Let's have a cup of coffee or something and I'll see where we're going.'

'There's some seats right here,' said Penny. 'We don't have to spend any more money.'

'I'm hungry,' Eric said. They ignored him and sat down to look at the *A to Z*.

'Attlee Court,' said Nick.

77

'That won't be there. Look for the street.'

He shoved Penny aside. 'All right. . .all right. I'll do it.'
Eric looked wistfully at a dazzlingly-liveried hamburger
parlour which was clearly not Empire made.

'Got it,' Nick said at last. He looked up from the book.
'Vauxhall.'

'Vauxhall?' Penny said. 'That's where they had the
Pleasure Gardens in Regency days. I read it in Georgette
Heyer.'

Nick ran his index finger down the tube map on the
back of the book. 'Easy-peasy. Don't even have to change
trains!'

Eric responded to the bright tone of voice. 'Well, I hope
he's there!'

There were no pleasure gardens at Vauxhall, that they
saw. There were adventure playgrounds however, that had
been beaten into submission by youthful high, or low,
spirits, and a lot of redevelopment which seemed to have
been suspended indefinitely at one stage or another.

Here and there were pockets of prosperity, and one such
was in the street they were looking for. Some deep brown
warehouses had been transformed into modern accommodation of some sort.

'This'll be it,' Nick said. He closed the street directory
and passed it to Penny, much as a naval captain might
relinquish his telescope to a junior officer.

She put it in the maligned shoulder-bag, saying, 'I told
you it'd be useful.'

'Yeah — this'll be it. It's like Docklands, isn't it. . .'

It was office accommodation, housing a great variety of
small companies.

'It's not flats,' Eric said, long after Penny and Nick had
realized this. 'That's flats.' He pointed down the street to
where a structure of pale, elderly concrete rose into the sky.

'That won't be it,' said Nick. 'It's not a Court.'

'I think it is flats, though,' said Penny.

'Well, we're walking in that direction anyway... But that's not it.'

The weighty concrete rectangle had a cavernous central lobby on the ground floor. On every other level of the building were concrete-balustraded walkways running past faded coloured doors. On the blank expanse of the forecourt there was a lopsided sign on stilts. 'ATTLEE COURT: UNITS NOW AVAILABLE.' Under this, in smaller letters, the sign continued, 'Attlee Court Housing Association' and gave a telephone number.

'Was council flats,' Eric said knowledgeably. 'Attlee is council flats. What number?'

The building did not fill him with dismay as it did Penny and Nick. They passed into the lobby, where stairs ran up to landings on either side. There was a powerful smell of disinfectant.

'Isn't there a lift?' asked Penny.

'Not in these ones,' Eric said. 'Just the stairs.'

They heard someone coming down the stairs now. Penny felt tense as the footsteps came nearer. A young man appeared on the landing above them, wearing one of those faintly military-looking anoraks. 'What do you want?' he asked as he came down to their level. He was quite well-spoken.

'My father lives here,' said Nick.

It might have been the password of today, for the young man continued out of the building without further comment.

'It's number thirty-nine,' said Nick. He would not look at his sister.

'I'll go first, if you like,' Eric said.

Nick pushed past him to the stairs. 'I'll go first.'

Eric stood back and remembered his manners. 'After you,' he said politely to Penny.

They came out on to the walkway on the third floor, where a light breeze was channelled into their faces like outdoor air-conditioning. There was a sequence to the flats they passed. Narrow frosted-glass window, door, wide window with partial or total lace-curtaining, then narrow window again. They heard traces of civilization from behind the windows: a gurgle of plumbing; a radio; a vacuum cleaner. Two of the doors had been drilled for spyglasses.

Number thirty-nine differed from the other flats only in the colour of the door; a pale green. Close up, one could see the door was hardboard over wood pulp. The hardboard had split in several places.

'He's not here,' said Penny, with certainty. Nick knocked on the door. Penny turned away and looked out at London over the concrete balustrade. She could see that a pub and an ugly Victorian church had survived the redevelopment. Between two relatively modern office blocks (or was one a hospital?) there was a glimpse of the Thames. She heard Nick knock again and Eric said, 'Nick. . .'

Something in his voice made her turn back. Eric had taken Nick's shoulder and was gently moving him aside. His big fingers tugged at something caught near the lock of the door. It was a few centimetres of a crushed packet of cigarette papers.

'It's been jammed shut,' said Eric, unsurprised. 'Do you want to go in?'

Nick swallowed and nodded. Eric gave the door a little short-arm punch with the flat of his hand and it sprang open. The mangled packet of cigarette papers held on to the door jamb for a second and then dropped.

Eric remembered his manners again, or perhaps he was suddenly nervous. 'After you. . .'

Nick and Penny edged into the hall. The kitchen was to one side of the front door and the bathroom to the other.

Both rooms had been torn apart. The bathroom cabinet had been ripped from the wall and the top of the lavatory cistern had been taken off. The kitchen cupboards gaped open, empty, and even the stove had been overturned.

Without speaking, Nick looked into the bedroom further

down the hall and Penny went on to the living-room.

The big window here let in plenty of light, so that the devastation stood out dramatically. A leatherette sofa, slashed. Light fittings torn down. An armchair skinned of its covers and pulled to pieces. A chest of drawers gutted.

The coffee table was undamaged. It was black and shiny with silver stars on it, and it caught the light as it lay on its side. Its legs were splayed out stiffly as if rigor mortis had set in. There was no other furniture and nothing hung on the walls.

'Oh no. Oh dear. Oh no.' Eric had come into the room behind Penny. 'Oh dear,' he moaned. 'Bother. This is bother. I mustn't get into any bother.'

'Shut up, Eric,' said Nick from the doorway.

'Oh no. Oh no. I mustn't get into any bother.'

Nick went back into the hall. Penny ran after him.

'Where are you going?'

'I'm going to shut the door,' he said quite normally.

'Oh no,' moaned Eric behind them.

Vincent, whose name was Melvin, picked some wax out of his ear with the top of a Biro. He examined this evidence of his existence.

'Hair. I've got hairy ears. I'm getting hairier, Col. Sign of age.'

'You can go deaf, sticking things into your ears,' Colin said.

Vincent again twiddled the piece of plastic in his ear. 'I could go mad sitting here. I know that.' He dropped the Biro top beside him. They had long ago stopped glancing across the street at the grey bulk of Attlee Court. Now they were waiting for a cue, any cue, to stop waiting.

'Here — look,' Vincent said, 'I just reached seventy thousand miles, Col.'

Colin looked at the mileage clock on the dashboard. 'Oh yeah.'

'Know what that means?'

'No.'

'It means we're sitting in a rust-bucket I couldn't even give away. That's nice to know, isn't it?'

Colin looked out through the windscreen, hoping to see a Jaguar car. He had seen three already while they had been waiting here and if he spotted another two he would have five hundred pounds, tax-free, every week for life. That was the deal he had made with himself. Of course, you didn't see many Jaguars in this part of Vauxhall, and that was the point: it mustn't be too easy to secure the money. It had to be a long shot or you wouldn't get it. Index-linked. It would go up in line with inflation. That was smart, he knew.

A meals-on-wheels van with as much mileage on the clock as Vincent's estate car went by them fast.

'See that? That's not her vehicle, is it?' Vincent said of the driver. 'So she beats the guts out of it. It's different when you're an owner-driver.'

'I want a car,' Colin said.

'You'll need your licence back first.'

'Yeah...'

It was a sore point with Vincent. A sidekick who could act as your driver as well as look heavy was something of a status symbol, but without his licence Colin became just another guy with a nose that had been spread sideways by boxing. What most infuriated the older man was that he now had to drive Colin around. He was not sure enough of his image to be wholly confident that the everyday punter might not simply take it that he was the driver and Colin was the main man...

Vincent had that pinched-mouth look again, Colin saw. He said, 'You'd get a couple of K for this motor any day.'

'You think so?'

'*You* would,' Colin flattered his mentor.

'Colin, the man who paid a couple of K for this would have so much hair growing out of his ears he'd look like a porcupine.'

They had passed a little extra time in this desultory discussion, since their speech was bulked out with swear-words. Vincent was thirty-five and his use of expletives was gracefully casual, but Colin was still close enough to his adolescence to invest them with feeling from time to time. It was involuntary—he knew it was wrong. Now he drew out a tin of hand-rolling tobacco.

'Don't do that,' Vincent said curtly. 'Reduces the re-sale value. You know that.'

'You just said...'

'Don't smoke in my motor—all right?'

Colin put the tin back in his pocket. 'He's not coming, Vinny. He's never going to walk in now. Not for days.'

Vincent looked up at Attlee Court. 'No. Maybe you're right.'

He made no motion to start the car, however.

'Don't do that, Eric,' Nick said sharply.

Eric was engaging himself in setting the furniture straight. 'It's dreadful...dreadful,' he said.

'Just leave it—OK?'

'I don't like it, Nick,' Eric said apologetically. 'It's upsetting. We might as well get it straight.'

'No. It seems to me that someone was looking for something. We should look too. There's no point in getting everything tidy.'

Penny was staring out of the window. She turned. 'Now what are you on about?'

Nick took his time in answering. Inwardly he was intensely excited. To him, this desperately dreary, ransacked flat gave out emanations of danger and romance. It was like a safe-house in a spy story. Somewhere where a man could hide out when his cover was blown... It couldn't be so, of course, yet the atmosphere was strangely stimulating.

'Listen, everyone,' he said to the two of them, 'we're

here now. What are we supposed to do — just get the next train home?' He enjoyed the authority he put into his voice. 'Call the police? Should we do that?'

Eric flinched.

'Don't play games, Nick,' Penny said. 'Don't start acting. This...this is *real*.' She began to stammer. 'It's...it's awful.'

Eric recognized her as an ally. 'It's dreadful,' he said. 'It's...awful. Dreadful.'

Penny went on, 'We've got to call the police. That's what you *do*.'

It was not what Eric did. She could read in his face that he felt cruelly let down.

'Yes, that's what you do *normally*,' Nick said. 'But I'm not going to do anything that gets my father arrested. *Shut up, Eric!*'

Eric had tried a bit of his breathing.

In raising his voice Nick rediscovered a tiresome truth, that the one who speaks loudest is likely to gain control of a situation. 'OK,' he breathed dramatically into the silence. 'OK... All I'm suggesting is that it seems more than just possible that someone was looking for something, so since we're here we might as well look too. The odds are...' he liked the sound of that so he repeated it, 'the odds are that we won't find anything. Fine. I know that. I simply suggest that we take it one step at a time, and the first step is to have a look around. And if we do actually find something that...that tells us something — well, we think again — we take it from there.'

'And when we don't actually find anything?' Penny asked.

Her brother shifted his ground. 'I don't think you care at all what happens to my father. Neither of you. Well, I do and I'm going to do what I can.'

'This is dreadful,' said Eric.

Vincent was Vincent because he hated being Melvin. At

school, 'Melvin' had become 'Vinny', and on his release into the adult world he had accepted 'Vincent' the moment it had been assumed to be his given name. It had a ring of class, he thought, and he had always had a soft spot for the Don McClean song 'Vincent', which had been played all the time when he was young. It wasn't the sort of song a hard man was meant to like, but it was really classy...Safe in Colin's ignorance, he hummed a line from 'Vincent' now... 'I could have told you, Vincent, this world was never meant for one as beautiful as you...' The song was about a painter who had cut off his ear. He would like to cut off Graham's ear. An awkward business, he imagined.

He murmured, 'When I see him, I'm going to cut him.'

Colin came awake beside him. 'What?'

'I see him, I'm going to cut him.'

'Oh no. You can't do that. Darkies do that.' Colin's racial prejudice ran so deep he never gave it a moment's thought. Vincent was more broad-minded.

'I got it from a black man, as it happens. That's just what he said. We was drinking in the Duke and he's all teeth and laughing and suddenly he says, "I see Sammy I'm going to cut him." He didn't say why... Girls? Money? He didn't say... He had one of these.' Vincent took from his top pocket a little device for cutting paper. An artist might use one. It was a tiny blade on a spring, contained in a plastic disc. He sprang it out and let it retract. 'He was a sharp dresser. Called himself Speedy.'

'You don't want to cut no one,' Colin said prissily.

'Drugs, probably. That would be his touch... I tell you, Col, this one I'm going to cut.'

Colin watched Vincent clicking the little blade in and out of the plastic disc. He supposed he'd have to hold the man, if that's what Vinny wanted. There must be an easier way of picking up money on the lump... He remembered, and looked out for a Jaguar car.

There were things you did and things you didn't do. You could have a good drink and get in a scuffle but you loved your mum and dad and you believed in Britain and you didn't use a blade. You had to go some way down before you carried a blade. Perhaps he was going downwards, with Vincent... Probably he must be. He looked at him. He was long and narrow, with big, practical hands. And that little mouth... How had he come to be running around with this? A chancer in a station-wagon with MOT troubles. Money...that was why.

He said, 'Are we going to wait here all day, or what?'

Vincent shrugged and drummed his long fingers on the wheel, feeling it vibrate to his touch.

'Are we?' Colin insisted.

Vincent gave him one of his best looks. The slow, dead-eye one. 'Why? Where you going?'

It would have to be me, thought Penny. It would just have to. The dog-eared business card read:

Need £££s?
No-Security Cash on Easy Terms
THE CREDIT SHOP
(Johnson-Spurling, Licensed credit brokers)

Under the printed address was handwritten the name Michael Golightly.

She had found the card adhering to the wainscoting behind the cooker. It had gathered fluff and that strange dark tar which builds up under cookers. Nick had found nothing but a few items of clothing, she knew. His murmurs of frustration had grown sharper and louder very quickly. First in the living-room and then in the bedroom. He had Eric with him to appreciate his sufferings. That was Eric's sole contribution, to follow Nick around, probably hoping as hard as Penny that nothing came to light that bore the faintest resemblance to a clue.

Well, this little card was hardly a revealing find, but Nick was sure to make something of it. It wasn't fair just to throw it away; and besides, there would then linger that fragment of doubt that it could have been important, or vital, even. Still, she rather dreaded his reaction all the same. . .

'Give it to me!' said their leader, the captain of the ship, the controller of spies, Mr Big, in that voice of authority that was so uniquely his, and — thought Penny — sounded so silly.

'All right. There.' She handed over the card.

'Where did you find this?' Nick looked at her keenly, as if the answer could well enhance the value of the clue.

'Behind the cooker.'

'Ah.'

She could see him studying the card. Not reading it — studying it. Eric wandered away from them in a minor state of distress. He too had a fair idea this grubby card spelt bother.

Nick mused, 'Credit broker. . . It all ties in, doesn't it?'

'I don't know,' said Penny.

'He needs money. This is one way of getting it.'

Unwillingly, she began to play the game. 'We didn't find any record of any business like that.'

'Even so. . .'

'It was behind the cooker. I don't think he especially treasured it.'

He missed the note of sarcasm and came up with a raddled beauty of a line. 'It's all we've got.'

'I should have just torn it up,' said Penny to no one in particular.

Graham saw the bonnet of Vincent's estate car protruding from the alley across from Attlee Court and stopped dead. The dirty silver bonnet of an old Granada with rally lights. What were the odds. . .

He turned away. He couldn't even get a change of clothes. He made an ululating noise in his throat. It went,

'Oh no no no no no. . .' There was no end to this. He had walked miles to get here. He was done in. No choice for it, he would have to sell the organizer whilst looking like a man who had spent the night in a park shelter. Now what would he get for it? And where?

The Elephant and Castle had a likely sound and it wasn't so very far; not for the experienced city-hiker he had become. . .

He ululated in misery again, 'Oh no no no no no. . .' as he shuffled away.

In Vincent's car they did not see Graham. But they did see a strange trio coming out of Attlee Court a few moments later. A boy led the way, in clothes that were marginally too big for him. He was holding out an open *A to Z* as if it was a forked twig and he was a water diviner. Behind him came an ill-assorted couple who managed to give the impression that they were walking more slowly than the boy, even though they kept pace with him. One was a man who could have been a regular visitor at the employment exchange and the other was a dull-eyed girl in a sensible raincoat.

Something about the boy held Vincent's attention. Colin did not look at them twice. If they weren't a Jaguar, he wasn't interested.

'Vinny. . .'

'Mmn?' Vincent's gaze left the little group.

'What's the cash-flow like?'

Colin saw Vinny's mouth zip up small again. He was going to make Colin ask straight out. He always did.

'It's been better.'

'I'm just about boracic,' Colin said.

'You always are, you.'

'What I mean — are you going to buy me a drink this week or what?'

Vincent milked the moment, remaining completely dead-pan for some seconds. Then, with a familiar flourish of his wrist, he brought out a roll of notes from an inner pocket. He snapped at two bills with his fingers, straightening them. The touch of the money made him feel powerful. 'Forty. Will that hold you?'

'Yes thanks,' Colin muttered. He hated this next bit.

Vincent played with the money some more. He folded the two notes tightly, like the first stage in some amazing display of Origami. This took a while. Then he tapped them into the top pocket of Colin's body-warmer as if they were a cigar. 'If you're going short you just tell me. Any time.'

'Yes. Thanks.'

'I been there. I know what it's like.'

'Yeah. Yeah — thanks.'

'Tell you what though,' Vincent said, reminded of it by the man in the old tweed jacket. 'You don't know you're born. When I started out, you had to sign on every week. None of this every fortnight and a month off at Christmas. You don't know you're born.' He smiled understandingly. 'Give it a couple of days, there'll be more, son.'

'Yeah. . .yeah. Thanks.' Vinny could keep it up for some minutes, this discussion of his generous patronage. Colin left a gap, to make sure today's session was over and then said more brightly, 'I thought I might have a drink tonight.'

'What else is new?'

'If you don't need me around.'

'Don't know yet.' Vincent looked at Attlee Court. 'I've had enough of this. We'll catch him later. I hope. . .'

He started the car. The waiting was over. Just like that. 'I'm going down the Mississippi.'

It was a drinking club, not an adventure holiday and Colin was enthused by the idea. 'Oh yeah. . .'

The car phone sounded. Vincent gave it a look of melancholy dislike.

'You don't have to take it,' Colin said hopefully.

'No.' But he picked up the phone. 'Yeah?' He listened to a man's voice talking urgently. When the man stopped speaking Vincent said, 'Where'd you get the plasterers,

Tommy?' He listened again. 'Sure I can make it, but it'll cost you. See you later.' He put down the phone and sighed. 'Give me strength.'

'Got a job on?'

'When I feel like it.' He looked discontented.

'We going for a drink, then?'

Vincent appeared to contemplate the idea. It was an act. He leant across and opened the passenger door. 'No. Sorry, Col — not going your way.'

'I could help.'

'No. Skilled work. Not this time, son.'

He left his status symbol standing in the alley. The tools in the back of the estate car clanked together as he drove off.

'You be at the Duke,' he called. 'I'll catch you later!'

CHAPTER 7

ON THE underground train the dirtied cable pipes in the tunnel appeared to snake up and down as the train burrowed onwards. Inside, the advertisements above the windows were motionless, in contrast to those you saw from an overground train or a car. The Londoner feels at home in this swaying limbo and Penny began to relax into the familiar stupor of the continual tube-traveller.

Nick looked at himself in the dark window opposite, where his blank face stared back at him as if from a film negative. Eric counted off the stations.

'Four more stops to go.'

The Credit Shop was in another area of London that was foreign to Penny. It was the kind of area in which those shops that are not discount stores have 'Genuine Sale' notices in their windows all the year round, and in many cases, 'Closing Down Sale: Final Reductions.'

There were so many people in the streets it seemed impossible that any shop could fail. Amongst the urban flak jackets and fatigues of these non-shoppers was the odd splash of vivid colour, usually a woman's raincoat, though some winter wear suggested that skiing was a popular pastime in the district.

The Credit Shop had no 'Sale' notice displayed. Nick led the way to the side street with his eyes on the oracular street guide, so that he could have been in Park Lane for all that he was aware of his surroundings. The building had indeed been a shop; a corner store. Now perpendicular strips of material formed louvred blinds behind its windows. The shop was so bland and businesslike that it hardly looked as if it was a place where one could ask questions which were of a personal nature. The investigators stopped on the other side of the street.

'Perhaps just one of us should go in,' suggested Penny, knowing it could only be Nick if that plan were adopted.

'No,' Nick said nervously. 'No, we. . .we have to present a united front. Anyway, Eric's got to come because he's the grown-up.'

'Oh, I don't know about that,' said Eric with feeling. 'It's really your business, not mine.'

Nick dropped his bombshell with the wanton innocence of someone who has tunnel vision in his pursuit of an objective. 'No — you've got to say you're our uncle. They won't listen to us on our own.'

'What?'

'You just say you're an uncle and you're here to see we get some answers.'

'I can't do that!'

'Why not?'

'I can't tell porkies! It makes me feel uncomfortable with myself!'

'You've got to,' said Nick simply.

Five minutes later they walked into The Credit Shop.

The oatmeal material of the blinds was repeated in the upholstery of the steel furniture, and the brown cord carpeting had a texture you could feel through your shoes. This part of the shop was a waiting-room, Penny saw. It was as impersonal as the room in which she waited to see her dentist. The difference was that here there was no reading matter of any description. One might at least have expected some literature explaining and extolling the services the shop offered, but there was none.

Instead, the shop's virtues were explained to them by a young black woman who was sitting there with a baby on her lap.

'What you here for?'

She was sullen and prone to abrupt, restless movements which disturbed her baby, although it made no sound, even when she raised her voice. 'You getting some money? Or giving it back?'

'Um — neither,' said Nick. He sat down with Penny, looking at the black woman. Eric stayed by the door and stared out of it fixedly.

'No,' said the woman. 'You don't want to, neither.'

'No?' said Penny politely.

'No. Lest you want to pay forty per cent and rising all the time. I do think it's at forty now. Then they add it on — what you don't pay.'

'Oh.' Penny wondered if the woman was drunk or whether she just had to talk. Either way she didn't make any sense.

'Know what I come here for? It was a television for the babies. I need for them to have a TV to watch. All the kids watch TV. He says, there you go now, no worries, and here I am paying, paying, paying. He going to have me on the streets — you know what I mean?'

Her voice was very loud. 'I just paying interest — know what I mean? I don't pay for the TV — no. I just give him money so he don't take what else I got. And I got no money in the first place. How you like that? Where I get time to work if I don't got no TV? Will you tell me that, please? You tell me please! Everyone got a TV. Yeah. Now I got one and that's all I got.' She brooded for a moment. 'That's very nice.'

At the door, Eric cleared his throat noisily. The young woman chose to take it as an interjection. She said to his back, 'Yeah, well. Your time will come. Your time will come. And I have told you.'

The door to what had once presumably been a stockroom opened and a grey suit came into the room. One noticed the suit because it was so sharply pressed that it might have been able to stand unsupported from within. The face at the top of it was as calm as the moon.

'Miss Armitage. You'd like to see me?'

'I'd like to see you? I'd like to see the back of you!' The

young woman enjoyed her joke hugely. 'I'd like that, man!'

The man stayed at the door. 'Would you like to come through?'

'He a funny man, isn't that right!' The black woman stood up and grinned at Penny.

'If you'd like to come through,' the man repeated in an accent as colourless as his suit.

'Oh, this is nice. . .' The young woman took her baby into the back office. The door shut behind them.

Penny gave Nick a faint, sick smile and thought he would read it as a smirk, until she saw the same smile of discomfort on his face too. Eric sat down now. He was quite unmoved by the woman's pain and defiance.

At first there was a period of comparative silence from behind the office door. When the woman began to shout the emotion that filled the resonating areas of her throat, chest and nose made it impossible to understand her. The words were hammered out so fast that a vibration set up somewhere in the walls or windows: the place was humming.

She kept on for some minutes. When she stopped the man spoke quietly for a few seconds, then she was back in at the same uncontrollable level of speed and sound.

The door opened and she was shouting, 'You take your hands off me! You don't hurt my baby! You don't hurt my baby — you're nothing!'

A grossly fat man had her by the elbow and was tugging her out with a series of sharp jerks. The needle was stuck on the record. 'You don't hurt my baby! You don't hurt my baby! You're nothing!'

They crossed the waiting-room and the man opened the door. He propelled the woman out and shut it. She set off down the street clutching her baby.

Penny realized the most shocking aspect of the whole horrid affair. Not once had the baby cried out in fear or anxiety. Either it was deaf or this was a normal day for it.

The fat man went back into the office without looking at them. Eric cleared his throat.

In another minute they might have recovered themselves enough to get up and walk out, but the office door re-opened almost immediately and lunar calm came into the room again. The man in the suit stood there regarding his visitors.

'Yes?' he said.

Eric cleared his throat. He stood up. 'I'm an uncle,' he whispered.

It was not the most surprising statement the man had ever heard. 'I see.'

It was Penny who stood up next, to her surprise. 'He's here with us.'

'Yes?'

'We wanted to see Michael Golightly.'

'That's me.'

'Oh.'

'About what?'

'Sorry?'

'What did you want to see me about?'

Nick got up now. 'My father. Um — his brother.' He indicated Eric with a nod of his head.

Mr Golightly turned his serenity on Eric. 'Yes? And what's your name?'

Nick said quickly, 'My father's Graham Hodge.'

'I don't reveal information about clients.' It was plain fact. 'But it so happens he isn't a client. . .'

Nick was disappointed. 'Oh. I see.'

'All right?'

Penny blurted out, 'No — we want to find him. We. . .we don't live with him but he's not. . .we don't know where he is.'

Mr Golightly pondered this without emotion. 'Would you like to come through?' he said.

He stood back so that the way into the inner office was clear. From what they could see, it was a featureless room, yet the thought of entering it was somehow very unpleasant.

Penny led the way. She noticed that the back of the door was quilted in mock leather. Inside, there was a desk, two filing cabinets and two chairs. This was a room in which two people talked across a desk. Or perhaps one of them might shout and scream abuse. The steel desk was bare of any papers or pens and the only wall-hanging was a courtesy calendar from a garage. Possibly even the filing cabinets were empty.

It was only when you came into the room that you saw it was subdivided into two and that you were not yet in the heart of the operation. A door led to another room which must house the fat man. And a secretary? Someone was rattling a computer keyboard with their fingertips.

Mr Golightly followed them in and shut the door behind him as a matter of course. They stood behind the visitor's chair as if it was a witness stand and he went to sit behind his desk. The window at his back was of stippled glass: there was no view to distract them.

Mr Golightly sat back and put the ends of his fingers together. He could have been a bank manager, Penny thought.

'Graham Hodge?' he prompted from his bottomless sea of tranquility.

Nick held out the grubby card. 'This was his. It's yours.'

'Yes.'

'We want to find him.'

Mr Golightly said to Eric, 'What's your part in this?'

'I'm...I'm just here,' Eric said.

The money lender kept his gaze on him for two or three seconds. He might well have been reassured by what he saw, because his attention shifted back to Nick. 'Brother and sister, are you?'

'Yes.'

'Looking for your dad...'

'Yes.'

Neither Penny nor Nick wanted to say more unless they had to.

An extraordinary event occurred: Mr Golightly frowned. 'It's a funny old world,' he murmured. His face reorganized itself. 'Well now.' He thought about what he would say next, unembarrassed by the silence he created. 'I can't really help you. There was a time when I thought your father and me might do a little business...He didn't want to.' He had no attitude to this; it was neither good nor bad. He thought a little more and it became clear to Penny that he was deciding exactly how much information he was going to let out. 'I ran into him a few times in the course of...business development. New business opportunities. In a difficult area of...'

Of what? London? Money-lending? Mr Golightly had said all he wanted to on that subject. 'He used a car firm,' he said. 'I wouldn't forget that. It made him a...figure. "Paula's Packages". North London. I think it was a North London firm.'

'Were you friends, or something?' Nick asked. He couldn't bring himself to believe his father would associate with this crushingly neutral human being, but with a horrible fascination he had to be sure.

Mr Golightly got up and went past them to the door of the waiting-room. He opened it. '*Yellow Pages*. Try the *Yellow Pages*.'

And that was all they were going to get. They filed out, Eric first, nodding and smiling his thanks, then Penny, then Nick.

On impulse Nick said, 'Thank you. I know you didn't have to tell us anything. Nothing at all. You didn't have to see us, even.'

Mr Golightly looked down at him and just for a second Nick thought he caught a glimpse of something quite dreadful in the man's eyes.

Compassion.

The spark of life faded. From far out in dark, dead space Mr Golightly said, 'Have a nice day.'

The visit to the Credit Card Shop had been a dreadful

disaster. So thought Penny as they scouted about for a main post office with a set of *Yellow Pages*. The element of disaster was the success of the visit. One clue had led to another, as Nick had hoped it would, and now it seemed that the act of taking this first step had irrevocably committed them to the next.

But this faint trail would probably peter out, or at worst lead on to a third step they could not contemplate for some reason... Such as...what? The good news was that they were only here for a single day. There was, mercifully, only so much you could do in just one day. Meanwhile they walked the High Street of this disgusting part of London looking for a post office. Penny had instituted a personal go-slow here. She had already complained she was tired and had already decided that if she spotted a post office she would not point it out. Why then did she feel so irritated with Nick that he had not thought of asking a passer-by?

What an awful area. They were passing a run-down cinema, which looked as if it had been moulded from ice-cream and sand. Steps led to a wide foyer, where the dirty glass doors gave the appearance of having been closed for a very long time. Plastered on the glass were strips of white card bearing day-glow writing in bold strokes.

'The National Game!' said one.

'Big Time Bingo.'

'£1 a Set—30p Gold Rush.'

'Traditional Bingo!'

'That's the Lot!'

Traditional? From the lofty heights of simple security, Penny reflected that these people had limited opportunities and little spare cash. Was it surprising that they should trudge out for a little monetary excitement? Of course, a lot of them would do the football pools, too... There, a helicopter rescue to a better life was available to them, if unlikely. Then a finger of panic ran down her spine as she remembered that this high ground of security which she took for granted had just fallen into the sea. In all probability it had only been an illusion in the first place. 'There we go!' said Nick. 'Post office!'

It was a building no one could have missed, a gleaming new bastion of bureaucracy in glass and stainless steel, and inside, on a black shiny counter, were pristine volumes of the *Yellow Pages*.

'Paula's Packages' turned up under 'Couriers' after a long search. The *A to Z* showed the address to be a fair distance from any tube station.

'North London Line,' said Eric. As Penny had with the travel-card suggestion, he couldn't resist showing off his knowledge. He added hastily, 'If you really want to go there...'

'We do,' said Nick.

'We should phone, shouldn't we?' Penny said.

'No. It seems to me that people aren't so likely to say "no" straight to your face. That's what we've found so far, isn't it?'

'Oh, you've got all the answers, haven't you.'

'I'm hungry,' said Eric.

They were all hungry. 'I don't want to go anywhere here,' Penny said with revulsion.

'We'll get a takeaway,' Nick decided.

It was by now almost three o'clock. Nick wanted a pizza, but here there were only burger bars, fish shops and kebab shops, and nothing stayed open after lunchtime. They settled for buying individual pork pies and some apples and fizzy drinks at an Asian grocery store. 'Have 'em on the train,' Nick said.

'Yes — much nicer,' said Penny.

The North London Line is an overground loop that starts at the Thames in the west of the capital and returns to it in the east. To Penny, who had never travelled it before, it held some of the excitement, if not the beauty, of a scenic railway.

They ate wondrously greasy pork pies and looked out

of the train windows on great tracts of London's backyard. The sights were not those one would show visitors.

Blackberry bushes and cowslip shared the embankments with a profusion of rubbish and the odd supermarket trolley far from home. Long, low brick buildings that might once have been factory and engineering works sat in asphalt compounds showing their grimed and shattered windows like mouthfuls of broken teeth. Some of these compounds were devoid of buildings and yet had barbed wire stretched around them on concrete posts. On others, heaps of tyres or bricks or iron girders surrounded corrugated iron sheds.

Nick and Penny were eating their apples as they passed by the great waste-metal yard at Willesden Junction, where unfathomable structures rose up like a derelict mine, looking like scrap metal themselves. Further on up the line wasteland supported stunted, wiry shrubs and trees and beyond these was a vista of Attlee Courts of every description, flying washing from their balconies like great ships signalling to each other across the ocean.

Middle class values and attitudes do not suffocate for a long time after the money-supply has been cut off, and Penny could not help but feel sorry for the families condemned to live in these high rise lairs without tumble driers. Surely the clothes must come in filthy from the line? She felt especially sorry for the unfortunates who had been allotted flats with pastel-coloured balconies. She glanced at Nick crunching into his apple. 'Isn't it horrid.'

His reply was as adult as you could get. 'Oh pull yourself together!' Shreds of apple flew out of his mouth.

'I just meant — '

'I know what you meant. Pull yourself together.'

Penny looked away, hurt. Nick took another gargantuan bite of his apple. He was feeling keenly the loneliness of leadership. No one else took any decisions: they just raised objections or complained. He knew that, given the smallest opportunity, Penny and Eric would turn around and take the next train back to Cambridge. Did they think he had no doubts? Did they think he was *enjoying* this? Well, of course he was, in a way... But running along parallel lines with his relish in the search was a yawning tunnel of despair and anxiety. He thought, 'It'll be better when I know what's happened to him.'

Tied on to this thought, jolting behind like an old tin can, was a little piece of doom: 'It won't, you know.'

If only none of this had ever happened. If only life had gone on unchanged. If only.

Penny had had enough of looking out of the window. Instead she turned to Eric, who was taking a small sip from his can of sparkling orange. He's making it last, she thought incredulously; he hasn't even started his apple yet. How childish could you get. But even so she envied him his ability to sit quietly inside himself with the engine turned off; not thinking, just being and making his picnic last...

'Eric,' she said conversationally.

'Mmn?'

'How come you know London like you do? Like knowing this train?'

His brain engaged and he began to think. 'Well...Penny!' It was the first time he had remembered her name and he was pleased with himself. 'Well, Penny,' he began again, 'I've been here before.'

'Well, yes, I know that, but...'

'I've lived in London, you see. I've been all over.'

'Doing what?'

'Different things.' He started to brush imaginary crumbs from the greasy jacket, uncomfortable now. 'I ran errands...I got around... Between being in the places I was in.'

She supposed he must mean institutions. What a tower of strength they had with them—honestly! 'Nick,' she said, 'what do you think we're going to find out at this place?'

'How do I know? I don't know. We wouldn't be going there if I did, would we?'

Eric polished his apple on his jacket sleeve. When he bit into it he was at once embarrassed by the noise it made.

They both watched, fascinated, as he tried to eat the apple in silence.

The address given for 'Paula's Packages' led them to a terrace of narrow three-storey houses which had been built shortly after the First World War and were less solid-looking than their late Victorian and Edwardian counterparts.

The brickwork on this house needed re-pointing and the plaster was crumbling around the gabled window on the top floor. On the door, a red resin plaque confirmed that this was indeed the home of 'Paula's Packages'. When Nick rang the doorbell there was only a rattling sound from inside the house and the bell-push came alive and tingled his fingers. The bell did not need to work any better than it did, because immediately a cacophany of sound welled up within the house. A dog's deep barking and the piercing excitement of very small children was switched on like a tape-recording. The dog reached the door first and settled into a monotonous series of single, coughing barks.

The door opened and the German Shepherd shot his head out and switched to some deadly growling. Behind it, a bony teenage girl held a baby in the crook of her arm, up by her ear. The baby was a model of its kind, jump-suited and with a face on which tears had cleared footpaths through food. Behind the girl was a mêlée of pre-school arms, legs and heads.

'What is it?' the girl asked shortly.

' "Paula's Packages"?'

'Yeah. What is it?'

'Is, um. . .is anyone here?' queried Nick through the noise.

'The cars are out all day.'

'Oh.'

'What did you want?'

'Paula?'

'She's gone to Birmingham. Back in the morning. Maureen's in Majorca. Holiday. All right?'

It was an unexpected setback. Nick was shattered. The girl started to shut the door.

'No — wait a minute!'

'What?' The girl kept the door ajar. The dog's head stuck out, growling still.

'Could you take a message?'

'If you like.'

'My name's Nick Hodge. I'm Graham Hodge's son.'

'Yeah?' meaning 'so?'

'Just. . .just say I wanted to talk about. . .talk about my father.'

'You want to talk about your father.' The girl waited to see if that was all the message was.

'I don't know where he is.' Behind him, Penny began to go red in the face.

'Come on, Nick.'

'Perhaps someone here knows,' he persisted.

The girl took in the idea, examined it and returned it undamaged by any opinion or comment. 'Do you want to leave a number?'

'I can't, really. I've got yours, though. I could ring.'

'So what shall I say?' the girl asked patiently.

'Say. . . Say I'll be in touch. Graham Hodge. That's who we're looking for.'

'Graham Hodge. All right.' The girl shut the door.

'I'm Nick Hodge!' Nick shouted at it.

They could hear the girl rounding up the children and driving them back down the hall. The dog had shut up. When Nick turned round to Penny and Eric he looked vacant, as if he had taken a heavy blow to the head. His search had come to a halt. Perhaps Penny should have leapt straight in and said, 'When's the next train to Cambridge, then?'; but Nick had engaged her sympathy and she could only echo his despair.

'What do we do now?'

Money.

Money. Notes. Each one a small sliver of self esteem returned. But, oh — just thirty pounds! Thirty pounds for a piece of equipment that had cost ten times that sum. . .

Graham had cleared the memory of the organizer before he sold it at a second-hand shop where electric guitars were a popular feature. He supposed he had been lucky to find anything open. The information in the machine still existed on computer disk at the cottage, but it had been a wrench, nevertheless. Still. . .he was solvent: he had options. . .

The option of going back to Cambridgeshire did not occur to him. He had to make the money work for him before he allowed himself to think of anything else. He was proud he had fought off the temptation to take a taxi as he ran up the stairs from the tube station to the street. And the sun was shining! He was still cold though, in his dirty suit. Eventually he would need to look respectable. But just now his intention was to be in a dark warm place where it did not matter: the temperance snooker hall across the road. . .

That would be the start. He was very hungry. It gave him a sensation of urgency, this physical need; a sharpness he must make use of before the day finished.

London was dark. Looking from the window of Graham's flat, Vauxhall looked particularly dark to Penny. In the distance countless star-like lights shone from a group of tower blocks. Below them the more important roads cast up a yellow glow which the gloom smothered before it could rise far.

It was six thirty and it didn't seem possible the day was only two thirds over. So much had happened. Waking in the cottage. . .Eric's house. . .Cambridge. . .the train. . .the search, which had been so enervating. . .Nick's 'logical decision' to return here to wait until it was time to catch the last train that would connect with a bus back to the village. . .

There was no television here, no radio and no phone. You could receive and send information and entertainment only by the human voice, to someone in the same room.

In the same room now, Nick and Eric were silent. They had all eaten another picnic meal, and plastic bottles and paper cups and crisp packets covered the star-spangled coffee table. The lights in the room were as subdued as those outside. It was something to do with the material of the shades and its effect was to double the dreariness of the flat after sunset.

Nick was sitting on the floor flicking at the plastic tops of the soft drink bottles. He had invented a kind of football game, aiming them at a goal formed by the legs of the coffee table.

Eric sat on the sofa with his hands on his lap. Over the minutes and hours his worried expression had washed away.

He was good at waiting. He had done a lot of it.

Graham came out of the temperance snooker hall with a bubble of euphoria in his gut and in his brain. He was now possessed of three figures: one hundred and fifty wonderful pounds. He had set this as his target at five o'clock and he walked out of the hall the moment the last notes were in his hand.

Now he must smarten himself up. There was a way; he'd done it once before when he was in a hurry. It had been a similar situation, with this feeling of running against the clock, working at full pace.

It was time to get a taxi. And see! There was a black cab motoring by at this very moment! His elation grew. Events were on his side. He had. . .*momentum*.

105

Graham paid off the driver at King's Cross. His purpose was so strong that he had no conscious knowledge that this was a place where one could board a train to Cambridge. *Momentum.* He could feel it like a huge hand at his back.

He was propelled first into a shop on the station which sold shirts and ties. And look — there was even a sale on! He bought a shirt with blue stripes and a red Paisley tie. God bless late night shopping and God bless the January sales, which started well before January. In another shop he bought a pair of socks. He still had well over three figures in his pocket. He dropped the socks into the carrier bag from the shirt and tie shop and went onwards.

To any observant traveller at the station he presented a curious sight as he strode towards the gentlemen's lavatory. He was walking so fast that he could have been in a speed-walking competition. He himself was unaware that he was creating this effect. He was aware only of. . .*momentum.*

He ran down the steps to the lavatory with perfect co-ordination, his legs working like pistons. Oh, lucky man — the shower cubicle was not only in service, it was empty.

The man engaged in relieving himself at the stalls paid Graham no attention as he went to the vending machine at the other end of the tiled space. Graham put in a pound coin and snapped out the drawer at the bottom. He removed from it the little box with a ribbon pictured on it, marked 'Stay-Away Pack'.

In the shower cubicle he went into a well-planned routine. Strip to the waist. Let the shower trickle water on to the dirty shirt. With the shirt, sponge down his jacket and trousers without making them too wet. Use a dry portion of the shirt to make a start on getting his shoes clean. No time for a relaxing shower: a 'bracer' was all he needed. . .

Now he wished he'd bought a pair of underpants. Too

bad. But the clean socks were the personification of luxury... Dressed only in his socks and pants he squatted down and opened the Stay-Away Pack. Inside their attractive casing the goods were utilitarian and looked downright cheap under the light of the cubicle. There was a flimsy comb and a razor and a pre-pasted toothbrush you slid from a tube, all in red plastic. The set was made up by three sachets with their contents described in four languages, one of which was Arabic. Shaving cream, after-shave, shoe polish.

He used the shoe polish first. It was a wet-strength synthetic handkerchief impregnated with silicone. It made his hands sticky but imparted an immediate lustre to those parts of his shoes that were still in a condition to accept it. Now he had to wash his hands again under the shower.

Time was slipping by. He noticed his fingers were trembling as he opened a second sachet. The after-shave on the towelette smelt like the cologne on face flannels in aeroplanes. It was not a smell he much appreciated, but since he was using it as an underarm deodorant it didn't much matter.

Be quick, be quick. Why are new shirts so thoroughly packaged? So many clips and strips of cardboard and cellophane...and pins... But he didn't prick himself because luck was running his way at last. On with the shirt. The buttons were stitched on so tightly... so hard to...nearly done. Put on trousers. Not dry but not too bad. Put new tie in breast pocket of shirt, just for now. All rubbish into the smart carrier bag, including old shirt, tie and socks.

Back out into the lavatory to the basins. Two more men were relieving themselves, interested only in their own bodily functions. Unusually, for a man shaving, Graham did not look at himself in the mirror any more than he must to perform the task efficiently. The toothbrush was strangely pliant and ineffectual, but he felt fresher for its use. Tie new tie. Hey—looked good. Finally he put on his damp jacket with that smartening jerk that men's outfitters use. Oh — comb hair...

Bingo. Ready.

He ran back up the steps into the station and threw the carrier bag into the first waste receptacle he passed. That too had a cleansing effect. It was as though by casting off his old clothes he had to some degree cast off his recent degredations.

Graham got into his stride and speed-walked out of the station. Oh, he was marvellously cunning, because now it was only a five minute walk to his objective.

In fact, at the pace he was going, he made it in three, to his surprise.

Some miles away, outside Attlee Court, the old Granada estate car crept backwards into the alley it had occupied earlier in the day.

CHAPTER 8

IN NUMBER thirty-nine Attlee Court Eric was asleep, slumped in the same position with his hands on his lap. Penny and Nick were talking. The lack of alternatives had forced this on them, but by now words came easily.

'Walking in here...'

'I know...'

'I didn't like going into the bedroom...'

'I know what you mean,' said Penny. 'It's a private sort of place, a bedroom.'

'Only it isn't, is it? Not here. That's what's so awful — it could be anyone's. I just can't imagine him sleeping there. I can't see it...'

'If you were a student, though, you'd think this place was great.'

'But he isn't a student. He's...' Nick did not know what his father was.

'Anyway,' said Penny generously, 'I think you did the right thing, bringing us to London. We had to do something.'

'Didn't get us anywhere, though.'

'Well, if the worst comes to the worst you can always call this Paula woman.'

'Yes. I suppose so.'

Now the day was nearly done it was so easy to say. 'The main thing is, you did the right thing. It was the right thing to do. It must make you feel better.'

'Well...I suppose it does.'

'Nearly time to go, isn't it?'

Nick looked at his watch. 'In a minute. Hey — look at old Eric. Wouldn't it be good if we just crept out and left him here!'

'It'd be horrid.'

'Yeah, but just think about it. Poor old Eric. I wouldn't do it, of course. Not for real...We could still be here, though — in the kitchen — just slam the front door?'

'No.'

'No. No... I wouldn't even do that.' He was feeling tired and mellow. 'Dad was a great one for fun and games. Do you remember?'

'Well...no.' Penny couldn't recall her father as a member of the household. Hardly at all.

'You don't? He was funny. There was a time — you'd have been about five — and you wanted to help with the laundry. Can't remember why Dad was doing it. Mum was on a course or something, maybe. Anyway, I came in and he was throwing the wet things across the room and you were catching them and putting them into the drier. Only he was throwing them too fast. They were all over you and you were laughing and laughing. So was Dad. You don't remember?'

Penny felt sad. 'No.' She cast back in her memory for a time when they had all lived together. When one came to her, it did not feature their father. 'I remember you and the cherries. You ate two pounds in one go. Mummy was furious.'

'Yeah. I still do that sometimes, with cherries. I love cherries. You don't start off thinking you're going to eat them all, but... You have a couple and they're nice, and then you think you'll just have one more, and then that one's not so nice. So you have another few, looking for a good one. You always want to end on a good one. But when you've just had a really good succulent one, you want another... I don't know how it happens, but you finish up just piling them in with both hands. You don't even have time to taste them, near the end.'

Silence crept back into the room. Nick fought it off for a moment. 'It was funny — you and the laundry. Laughing and laughing...'

The front door crashed open and there were footsteps in the hall. Penny and Nick were immobilized by shock. Identical thoughts filled their minds: this was not their father; they should never have come back here.

Eric came to his feet in a daze, conscious that someone had come in and he was an uninvited guest in the flat. The next moment two men were in the room. Both parties were very surprised at what they saw and Penny had a second or two in which to take in the appearance of the two men. The one who had come in first was tall and narrow with dark hair and square hands like garden forks. He wore a blue business suit. The other man was burly and looked bigger still in a body-warmer worn under a blouson jacket. His features were blurred, like a work in bronze that stopped just short of being an exact likeness.

Penny and Nick stood up. Penny clutched at her bag as though she absolutely refused to be mugged. Vincent and Nick spoke at the same time.

They said, 'What are you doing here?' in rather different tones of voice. In that instant it was like a scene from a situation comedy.

Then Vincent said, 'Shut up. What are you doing here?'

In his fear Nick could think of nothing but the literal truth. 'Just waiting.'

'Yeah?'

'Yes. We were just going, actually. Got to get a train.'

'I've got to get home,' Eric said urgently, 'I mustn't get into any bother.'

'Keep him company for a minute, Col,' said Vincent. Without quite knowing why, he kept his eyes on Nick.

Colin was drunk, but he was used to that and it did not show. He walked to Eric with a relaxed, bouncy step. He knew the exact distance to keep between them and when he got there he stopped and balanced himself, poised for a scuffle if that was what Eric wanted. He said in a friendly way, 'Take it easy, all right?'

His eyes were watchful and they made Eric nervous.

'I've got to get home. I don't live here,' he said, as if it was confidential information and Colin would understand.

Vincent took his cue. 'Yeah, I know they don't live here. So what I want to know is. . .' and he walked towards Nick and Penny, not minding how close he got, '. . .what are you doing here?'

He looked down at them without expression. It was creepy.

'I told you — we're not doing anything!' Nick said.

Vincent stared at him, willing him to feel small. Then it came back to him. This was the strange trio he had seen those hours ago, walking past the car. It came to him too, that there was something about this kid that was familiar. . .

Penny made her break for it, running to the door.

Vincent threw out a hand to grab her, but he had been standing too close and missed. The moment his attention was distracted Nick ducked past him as well.

'Colin!' Vincent bawled. 'Get them!'

Colin thought it would be far more logical if Vincent did the getting and he hesitated. Eric said, 'I've got to go,' in a way that suggested he had to use the lavatory and shoved Colin.

Colin fell over the star-spangled table and grabbed at Vincent's jacket in his fall.

'Get up!' Vincent shouted. 'Get up!'

Penny and Nick were out of the front door now and Eric had reached it himself. 'No. . .wait!' he called. 'I'm coming too!'

From behind him came not pursuit, but a barrage of expletives from Vincent. Colin had him by the arm. 'What's it matter — let 'em go.'

Vincent tore himself loose. 'That's his son! They're his kids! We're going to get them and they're going to talk to us!'

He ran out of the room towards the open front door. Colin contained an upsurge of beer into his throat and jogged after him. A chase. A bit of fun.

On the walkway outside he had to increase his pace. Vincent was really serious about this.

The reluctance to ask directions of a stranger is a very minor curiosity compared to the barriers to communication which slam down when danger threatens. Not once did Penny or Nick think of shouting out for help or banging on doors. In their terror they felt as alone as if they had been lost on Dartmoor. Fear caused them to lose rhythm in their flight and their shoes slapped down on the stairs in irregular patterns of sound. Behind them Eric kept pace easily and so surprisingly quietly that they forgot all about him.

They raced out on to the courtyard. Suddenly London seemed far too well lit. 'Tube,' gasped Nick and ran on. For several terrible seconds it appeared to Penny that he would break clear of her. She grabbed her shoulder-bag to her chest and ran after him for all she was worth.

When Vincent and Colin charged out of Attlee Court their prey was a good two hundred metres ahead of them. Vincent knew exactly what to do. Years of exposure to American movies with night-chase sequences made him reach into his pocket for his car keys. As he and Colin arrived at the old Ford, he discovered the first difference to the movies. You didn't jump straight into your vehicle and drive off: you fumbled to open the door and then you fumbled with the key in the ignition. Meanwhile your partner wanted the passenger door unlocked for him and you weren't driving a souped-up Chevvy but an old Granada which was reluctant to start.

Had he known it, however, the moment when the car finally swung out and its headlights shone down the street had precisely the effect it had in the movies. Penny and Nick stopped for a second and looked back and despaired. Thoughts of reaching the underground station left them. The imperative became to get off this long straight road they were sharing with a pursuing car. To their right was a fenced-in building site and immediately to their left a narrow road servicing industrial premises from a bygone era. Without thought to the consequences, Nick ran into its blackness. Following, Penny regretted his choice. Here there were no street lights except at the very end of the road and the thought of being caught here, in the dark, terrified her. And just when they needed some gaps in the urban surroundings there were none. There were no side alleys here and no development.

It became increasingly plain that their only hope was to run the length of this dim Victorian ravine and trust for better luck at the other end. Penny's impression was of tearing past a continuous wall of mouldering brickwork broken by a series of huge metal doors that had rusted themselves shut forever.

The headlights swept around the corner behind them. The car could not fail to catch them. As they heard the engine accelerate, Eric overtook them easily, as if the sound came from his own personal two point eight litre engine. With a pacer in front of them they found they could run even faster.

In the Granada, Vincent was trying to get his rally lights to work. They just wouldn't come on and unthinkingly he relaxed his foot on the accelerator pedal. 'I don't believe it! Would you believe it!'

'What?'

'I wired them myself! I don't understand it. . .'

Nick's chest was hurting. His lungs seemed to have shrunk to nothing. The street lamp at the end of the lane grew larger in his vision. It was a miracle that the car hadn't yet caught up with them. Ahead of them Eric leant to his right and hurtled round the corner like a football player swerving away from a mob of opponents. When Nick and Penny made the turn he had gone. Immediately they turned sharply to the right again, as he had done. The last building in the road was wedge-shaped: another street cut back in almost the same direction they had come from. The headlights of the estate car lunged around the first corner and kept going straight on.

Eric again changed direction, going left down another

street and into an even earlier period of history. A long stretch of iron railings fronted a row of houses which had existed long enough to have been placed under a preservation order. Steps led up to their front doors and more steps disappeared down to a semi-basement level. At the end of the street was a public house and the sounds of a juke box playing Country and Western music.

Eric did not look back as he stopped running and tried the side gate of one of the houses. It was locked. He took hold of the next gate he came to and it swung open as Nick and Penny caught up with him. 'No!' Nick panted. 'Keep going!'

'No. Listen.' He was breathing deeply but he was not as physically distressed as Penny or Nick. They listened and heard the unmistakable high engine note of a car reversing at speed.

'They're coming back,' Eric said softly. 'Come on.' He went down the stone steps very quickly. Nick paused to shut the heavy gate as quietly as he could before he followed Penny down. At the bottom of the steps there was a barred window, a door and some dustbins. They flattened themselves against the wall just below street level.

'We're trapped here!' whispered Penny.

'Shut up. Someone might be at home,' Nick whispered back. He looked at Eric. The gardener was listening to the car. For some reason of concentration or shock he did not seem as upset as Nick expected him to be.

A story in sound unfolded. The big car slammed to a stop in reverse and screeched forward. After accelerating for some metres it slammed to a stop again and laboured backwards. Then it wrenched itself round and tore down the street they were in. They heard it travel the length of the street and slow to turn the corner by the pub.

The sounds of the motor receded. Penny's legs were shaking uncontrollably.

'Come on, then,' Nick said in a low voice.

Eric's hand sank into the soft leather jacket and pulled

him back. 'I don't think that's a good idea,' he whispered laboriously.

'We've got to get to the tube! We've got a train to catch!'

'That's not very clever, Nick.'

'We've got to get home!' The isolated cottage seemed a haven now.

'Well, I'd like to get home too. This is dreadful. But if those men want to find you, they could be driving round here a bit more. And one of them could be waiting where he could see the tube station and the bus stops. I thought I should tell you that. It's very worrying.'

And all too likely, Penny thought. 'What did they want?' she asked.

'Nothing we could give them, anyway,' Nick said. 'How much money did you bring with you, Eric?'

'I've spent mine already.'

A second ago Eric had appeared really quite adult. This reply shredded that illusion.

'You've *what*?'

'Well, we were going home weren't we. I didn't need much.'

'We do now — we'll have to buy new tickets now,' Nick said, horrified.

'Oh,' whispered Eric. 'How much did you bring?'

'Well, actually, I've just about spent all —'

They froze. A light had come on behind the barred window. The curtains that saved them from detection were like old tea towels, un-ironed and so faded and worn that a great block of light charged out to illuminate the three interlopers.

Above them came the sound of a car driving back slowly, seekingly, along the street.

They shrank back into the wall and waited for discovery from one side or another.

Graham's entire nervous system drank in the ambience

of the One-Eyed Jack Casino. He was in his element in the muted lighting, listening to the soft and delicious clack of the gaming chips, as a lizard is at home on a hot rock.

The patrons' exclamations of euphoria or disgust, when they came, were an intrusion; these people did not understand that, come what may, the atmosphere should be still and relaxed, so that the inner excitement had space to breathe and grow.

Of course, the One-Eyed Jack was an inferior establishment. The name alone told you that. But the betting limits were right for this stage in his fortunes and his faintly disreputable appearance did not count against him here. As long as he had money and wore a tie he was acceptable.

So far he had been cautious in his lust. Sweet agony, while all the time the *momentum* wound up inside him, begging for release. When the feeling was right, it would be the blackjack table, he knew.

The estate car cruised aimlessly through Vauxhall, returning from time to time to the area around Attlee Court. Colin didn't see the point of it.

'They'll be miles away by now.' He wanted to go home. The pubs were shut: the day was over.

'He didn't say anything about kids,' Vincent muttered resentfully.

'Why would he?'

'Divorced — that's all he said. Little toe-rag.'

'Oh, leave it alone.'

'He took me, didn't he. All the way. I should've known when we lifted him home that first time. "Only temporary, while the divorce goes through." He's got nothing — not living there — he couldn't have. Why did I believe him?'

Colin could have reminded him that Vincent had been very willing to believe Graham's projected image as a man of means because he wanted to take his money. It didn't seem the moment, though.

117

Vincent put it another way. 'How could I let someone so soft muck me about like that?'

'Well...you should stick with what you know,' said Colin wisely.

Vincent's dead-eye look abandoned him. 'What do you know about it?' he said in an anguished snarl. 'You know *nothing*.'

'I tell you one thing I know — you don't take markers.'

Vincent was honest enough to admit the truth of that. 'Yeah. I was too sure about it. He looked so soft. What I should've done — I should have gone with him.'

'Yeah...but he didn't have any money to pick up in the first place, did he? So you wouldn't have got nothing.'

'I would have got...satisfaction,' Vincent said with dignity, as if he were an eighteenth century duellist. 'As it is, I look a complete prawn.'

'Yeah, well... Thing is, he's done a runner.'

'Mmn...' Any minute now he would turn for home. The whole incident had been like dropping a five-pound note in the street: you had to return to the spot and do what you could before you forgave yourself. The loss of face still rankled, but Vincent was beginning to feel he could cope with the financial loss involved here.

Colin put it very nicely, 'You win some and you lose some...'

The banality made Vincent's discontent flare up again. He drove on at an even speed for a good minute longer before he said, 'Life's too short and you're long time dead,' and pressed down his foot on the accelerator.

The light had gone off. No one had opened the door to put out rubbish or milk bottles. For reasons of security you didn't have things delivered around here. It had been a long time since they had last heard the slow searching note of the Granada's engine. It had been very unpleasant for the first half hour. After that they had begun to feel comparatively safe. Now Nick took the initiative. He felt it was time to reassert his authority. 'What d'you think?' he asked, more nervously than he intended. His voice squeaked like a badly-tuned radio.

'Ssh!' said Penny.

'We could stay here,' whispered Eric.

'Don't be ridiculous. I'm going to have a look.' Nick crept up the stairs. The street was as empty as its silence had led him to believe. Up here on ground level there was a breeze and it seemed far colder.

'Come on!' Apart from anything else, they needed to talk and they couldn't conduct a conversation outside what might be someone's bedroom.

Penny came up the steps quietly and joined him; then Eric, who shut the gate behind them.

'It's *cold*,' said Penny.

'Yes — quite warm down there, it was,' agreed Eric.

'I hope you don't want to go back to that flat, Nick.'

'No, Penny, I don't. That'd be stupid. Come on — walk.'

'Where?'

'Anywhere.' They walked towards the silent and darkened pub. 'All right, Eric,' Nick said grimly. 'You didn't bring any money, you said.'

'Well, not much, no.'

'Cheque book? Card?'

'I do have a cheque book but I just brought what I needed, Nick. For one day. And I've —'

'I know. You've spent it. What've you got, Penny?'

'I don't know — about five pounds, maybe. You made me buy all that food, remember?'

'Only because I'd just about spent all mine. You had more than me.'

'You just splashed money about the whole time — whenever you felt like it.'

'No, I didn't. Anyway, it's not worth arguing about. It's tomorrow now and all our tickets are useless. We've got to think.'

Penny stopped walking.

'I'm tired, Nick. I've had enough.'

'How extremely helpful.'

'I'm sorry. I just want to go to bed.' She began to cry. She was so tired she was quite unselfconscious about it.

'Hey — look — I'm sorry, Pen.' Nick put his arm round her. She cried more.

'It's just... Those men...and no money...and I'm so tired...'

'I didn't bring a toothbrush,' Eric said suddenly. Penny suspended her tears. She and Nick looked at each other.

'I brush my teeth regularly. I've got a routine.' He was talking more to himself than to them. Faced with Eric's anxiety attack, tears seemed inappropriate. Instead, Penny put her arm around Nick's waist. He wasn't a very substantial figure to cling to, but the contact made her feel better.

Eric went on a little wander. 'Oh...this...this...I don't know — this is just dreadful. I can't wash, I can't brush my *teeth*...I keep myself clean these days. This is...' He came over to Penny and Nick. 'You're a nuisance. You're silly,' he said bitterly. 'I brush my teeth regularly.' His eyes glittered with ill-feeling.

He's gone quite mad, Penny thought. He hasn't seemed to mind most of what's gone on today and now he's in a state because he can't brush his teeth.

Nick was more used to Eric. He disengaged himself from Penny and got right up close to his friend. 'Look, Eric. None of us can brush our teeth. It's not just you. We're all in the same position. And now Penny's had it and we've got to find somewhere to sleep. That's what we've got to do — isn't it, Pen?' Penny nodded. 'We don't have to think about anything else just now. Forget about brushing our teeth: all we need is somewhere to sleep. Have you got any ideas?'

Eric looked at the suffering Penny. 'But what are we going to do tomorrow?' he asked. He was calmer, though.

'Forget about tomorrow. We just want somewhere safe and warm to sleep. You see, we need your help.' A masterstroke, he thought. He began to stamp his feet on the pavement, fighting the cold air.

'We could go home — to my home,' Penny said unevenly. 'Only it's miles away and we haven't got enough money for a taxi. . .' She started crying again. Nick tried to make use of the interruption.

'See, Eric? Penny's much worse off than we are.'

'Yes. I can see that. Somewhere to sleep. . . And we don't want any more bother, do we?' He was very earnest about that.

'No,' said Nick equally earnestly, since it was the required response.

'All right. Follow me. If we stick near the river I'll find us somewhere. I'll get us there. Don't worry, Penny.'

It seemed natural for Nick to put his arm around Penny again.

They followed Eric. He said, 'I can get us near the river. That's first. We'll be all right, Penny!'

He wished he still had his organizer. Not that he would have used it here, but it gave him a psychological boost: he was a businessman, supported in the conduct of his business by scientific principles and state of the art technology. A shuffled pack of cards was only a random succession of the numbers between one and fifty-two, and Graham had evolved a system of possibilities and probabilities. He knew that although blackjack was the biggest earner for most casinos it was also the game at which a handful of professional gamblers made a good living. The basic principle was to reduce the luck factor — the random nature of the fall of the cards — by a method of card-counting. In Graham's personal scientific system the gambler's instinct was allowed some house-room; because he could not suppress it.

Experience had shown him that his biggest wins had come from instinct. He had a less clear recollection that his biggest losses had come from the same source.

Tonight he had very little stake-money and he must apply all his skills, however infallible he might feel just now. The first stage was to let the pattern of play enter his unconscious mind. Then, before he entered the game, he would attempt to banish all emotion and count a few cards. *Then...*

The cards became very large as he focused on them. It was a good sign.

The broad steps could have led up to a cathedral.

They had arrived at Waterloo station and the clock above the entrance told them it was one thirty in the morning. Their bodies told them they were very cold and very tired. The coldness increased in direct ratio to their fatigue.

'Not much further,' Eric said. He still had life in his step. Perhaps it was because he knew where they were going. Penny and Nick had reverted to a younger age, where you went with your elders without question or interest.

He led them away from the station and down into an enormous concrete basin. There were so many entrances and exits to the murky pedestrian concourse that it could have been designed as a gathering place for giant rats. Vehicles had access if necessary; an ambulance was parked near the centre, by one of a number of red metal benches. As they passed the ambulance they saw it was marked 'Mobile Surgery'. It was as if it had been abandoned after a joy-ride; there was no one in it or near it. Further on, where the sunken circus ran under the streets, there were people. They stood or sat amongst the fat pillars of ribbed concrete which supported the weight of the traffic when there was any. Round lights were set flush in the heavy ceiling as though they had been fixed expressly in order to filter down their dispiriting beams on to this outpost of Cardboard City.

Cardboard City. Penny recognized it from the kind of television documentary her mother searched out at off-peak viewing hours. This...*this* would be the safe warm place Eric knew. What were they thinking of, to let themselves be led by this half-wit? They were continually deceived by his adult exterior, even now... Well, perhaps especially now, when they were exhausted. At Penny's side, Nick looked suspiciously at the waiting figures under the dismal overhead lights. 'How much further now?' he asked.

'We'll just see where we can fit in,' Eric said.

Nick's mind was as tired and numb as the rest of him. It wasn't until they were in under the grey ceiling that he said, 'Not *here*, Eric!'

'Safe as houses here. You get something to eat if you're lucky. Do-gooders. Mind you, a lot of them just want to ask you questions. You have to be lucky.'

The men and women who lived rough here had no curiosity about Eric and his companions. Plenty of young people passed through here.

When Nick saw the cardboard boxes lined along the walls and wherever it was dark, his revulsion strengthened. 'No — Eric — not here! I'm not sleeping here!'

As he spoke he registered that the cardboard boxes that were used as individual coffin-like shelters were nearly all of similar size. Perhaps there was an ideal for this form of habitation — or maybe it was just that a batch of boxes had turned up from the same manufacturing company — one that made refrigerators, possibly.

Naturally Eric was hurt. 'If you've got no money this is the best place and we were quite near.'

Nick said, 'I'd rather we'd stayed where we were.' He spoke in a fierce whisper; he didn't want the homeless people around him to think he was insulting them. Not that they looked at all dangerous, which was in itself an oddity.

123

'Yes, well, I said it was warm there, didn't I, but you didn't want to stay.'

There must be almost a hundred people here tonight, Nick calculated, and at least ten were teenagers. He was surprised to see dogs in the encampment. 'Keep moving,' he urged. 'Just keep moving!'

'We won't find anywhere better.'

'I don't care.'

Penny had come to know her brother pretty well. 'May as well go on, Eric.'

'He asked me for my help,' Eric said stubbornly. 'I think we should stay here.'

A short-haired mongrel dog came up to them. Its tail flicked from side to side, yet its eyes were wary. When Eric bent down to pat it, the dog recoiled and ran off to a girl who was standing watching them from a distance of about twenty yards. She was in her early teens and had on a filthy grey parka and track suit trousers which were too big for her. Eric smiled at her, embarrassed by the dog's reaction to him. She smiled back in an everyday way and Nick had the sudden fear that she would come over and talk to them, or beg for money. It was not the idea of refusing to give her anything that worried him, it was the unfathomable dread that by talking to her they would somehow be sucked down into this hopeless subculture.

'*Please*, Eric,' he implored softly.

'You don't know about these things. There's hostels for your age, if you've got nowhere or you've run away. People come round here and get you into them.'

'No,' Penny said. 'Then you get questions and the police. We'll just keep going. It was a good idea, though,' she added.

That mollified Eric. To Nick's relief, he started walking again.

'I'll put my thinking cap on,' he muttered.

No, the people here weren't dangerous. You could look at them all you wanted to and they didn't get resentful or angry. Like the animals in the zoo, they were used to being looked at. There were drunks here too, though, and they would be more volatile. . .

They kept walking, through the people and the pillars and the boxes, under the perpetual neon dusk. A picture formed of a tribe of sleeping and slow-moving people who seemed to have all swapped clothes in some stage of their existence here.

Eric led the way out up a ramp like one in a multi-storey car-park. 'We'll cross the river,' he said, 'try there.'

As they ascended they saw a last row of cardboard boxes in the gloom beneath them. Probably these terraces of boxes were created to share body heat rather than as a purely social arrangement.

Nick said, 'I'm glad that's over. We're well out of there.'

'It's not over,' said Penny. 'This goes on all around the South Bank.'

'Does it? Well, we're going over the river soon.'

Penny was too tired to suggest to him that the river wasn't the Jordan and north of it wasn't the Promised Land.

Two years ago, in a moment of triumph, Graham had been barred from a gaming club in Cambridge because of his regular successes. Tonight he was in no danger of attracting the attention of the management in this way, but he had already doubled his money and was wondering if it was time to get a taxi and move on to a classier place.

Then the dealer caught his eye and smiled at him. It was a sympathetic, understanding smile. No—he would stay here. Although the man was only in his twenties the bags under his eyes hung down like water gourds. He was tired. Graham was tired too, but his concentration was still sharp. He would stay here, where his luck was good.

He smiled back his own tired, sympathetic smile. They were both professionals, after all.

CHAPTER 9

'NOT IN there. Policemen look in those.'

It was a telephone engineers' tent, about the same size as a Punch and Judy tent and similarly striped. For a second Penny thought of Eric's dream days at the holiday camp. *Fun at the pool.* . . Like a line from a song, it was one of those phrases she couldn't shake off.

'I'm so cold,' she whispered.

The night wind blew fitfully. 'Rain soon,' Eric said. He kept walking. The north bank of the Thames was also littered with people sleeping rough, and all the best spots were taken.

They ended up in a kind of courtyard at the back of a tiny restaurant near the Middle Temple. 'Where it's quiet,' said Eric. There was an ageing smell of garlic and wine; and all around them the inhuman tranquillity of the British judicial system, to which this area belonged, mind and soul.

Nick, the country boy, had a tourist's image in his brain as he plummeted into deep sleep. When they were crossing the Thames he had seen the floodlit Houses of Parliament. The intricate buildings had been so perfectly displayed against the indigo sky that they had seemed to be a miniature construction in matchsticks. All the view needed was a celestial piece of sky-writing: 'Greetings from London'.

As his face relaxed into the coarse concrete on which he lay, it began to spot with rain.

Penny was curled up against a wall. The wind threw raindrops at her. Eric got up self-importantly.

'Shelter, Penny. Shan't be a minute. Stay just where you are.'

Beyond fear or loneliness Penny fell asleep before he came back.

It was still dark when she woke up with a damp weight on her. Cardboard. Evidently Eric had gone on a search for the life-preserving substance and evidently it had rained harder. The broken-up cartons were saturated, but under them she was almost warm, if damp. When she cast aside the cardboard condensation rose from her like steam.

Nick and Eric were talking. Nick's hair was wet and lay tight to his scalp. 'We can hitch a lift back. That's not a problem.'

'Cars wouldn't stop for me, Nick,' Eric said. He had a stubble of beard-growth, Penny saw. She sat up, still steaming.

'What's happening? What's the time?'

'It's six o'clock. We've got to get moving, Penny,' Eric said. 'There'll be people here soon.'

Nick said, 'The question is, move to where.' He anticipated Penny's interruption. 'We've got nothing to lose by going back to that parcels place. We might as well be there and have no money as be here with not enough to get us home.'

'You're not thinking ahead, Nick,' said Eric.

'There isn't anything ahead,' Nick said bleakly. 'Nothing.'

Penny tried to wake up a little more. She felt dirty and itchy and scratched at her collar bone. 'I know where we can get some money,' she said.

Nick and Eric looked at her with astonishment. 'Really?' asked Nick.

'Yes. I should have thought. Mummy has this big spaghetti jar. She puts coins in it — saving up for charity. Help the Aged, I think it is at the moment.'

'How much?'

'Well, it's pretty full. She waits till it's full to the top. There could be thirty or forty pounds. More, maybe. We could take enough for our fares back, for sure.'

'We could take it all,' Nick said fervently.

127

'Well, yes. . .'

'Come on, then!'

'All right.' They got up stiffly. 'There's a bus that goes right to our door, during the day,' Penny said. She had stood up too quickly and was giddy.

Eric asked, 'How do we get in?'

'Key under a flowerpot.' She began to feel a small bump of optimism about today. Nick ironed it flat.

'Paula first.'

'What about breakfast?' Eric asked.

'No.'

Across the river in Battersea, the delivery van dithered along ahead of him like a sick cockroach and Vincent flashed his lights and blasted his horn. He was resentful at being up at this hour. High-rollers rose late and took time to put on their gear: electricians threw themselves into their overalls and hit the road without even having breakfast. . .

The van made space and Vincent surged by.

'Early start, Vinny. Be there,' Tommy had threatened. And yesterday he'd taken exception to a couple of Vincent's little professional shortcuts. What made Vincent furious was that Tommy had been in the right.

Well—who cared? Life was too short and work was only a means to an end. And the objective was, an end to work itself. Underneath his blue overalls, like a butterfly in a baggy chrysalis, was Vincent the playboy gambler, a man you didn't mess with; a careless creature who could go where he pleased when he pleased and stay there just as long as he wanted to.

In the meantime he was late for work.

Nick's argument had been almost unassailable: there was just enough money for fares both to 'Paula's Packages' and then on to their mother's house. Until they reached there they would have to do without food. It all seemed logical, but they were hungry already.

In the tube train they joined other people going about their business in anti-social hours. Many of the travellers were black and at least two were disabled. Trying to guess the nature of their employment, Penny concluded that the majority would be office-cleaners and labourers. Some of them read tabloid newspapers which carried gargantuan and, to her, quite incomprehensible headlines. The handful of City businessmen travelling with them appeared to have been unnecessarily savage in their morning ablutions, as though they had gone through a car-wash. Their skin was shiny and they read broadsheet newspapers with an air of contained impatience.

After almost an hour in the twilight world of the underground railway system it was unsettling to be released into a world that was still dark. It was raining again and in the wet the traffic sounded heavy, louder than usual. The station was situated under a blackened brick railway bridge and Penny stopped Nick from marching out from under its shelter.

'We can't, Nick. We can't turn up while it's still dark. Be sensible.'

'Yes...OK.'

They waited, dumb, under the bridge while the traffic increased and the warmth of their subterranean journey left them and their damp clothes became chilly. By slow degrees the rain appeared to dilute the inky blue of the sky and after half an hour they all three squatted down against the brickwork, feeling a strangely sweet lethargy in their legs. With a cap before them on the pavement they would have looked like beggars. Their heads drooped and they were mindless of the passers-by. Gathering numbers of legs and wheels passed across their line of sight.

At eight o'clock Nick said, 'She's got children. She'll be up by now. We daren't risk missing her.' He stood up and started off. Penny trailed him by a few metres. She didn't care by this time; all she wanted was to be back in her own home with her arm up to the elbow in the spaghetti jar full of coins. Eric fell into step beside her, looking vacant, as though his mind had emigrated even further than hers, to Cambridgeshire. The street lights were still on but the traffic had thickened and hissed onwards more slowly down the street, making a sticky sound on the glistening macadam.

By the time they reached the house Nick was quite a way ahead of them. The slight electric tingle rang into his elbow as he pressed the bell; the dog gave voice. Upstairs, small children squealed. Penny and Eric reached his side as the door opened.

Paula of the Packages looked like a badly-wrapped parcel herself this morning. Over cord trousers she wore a brown smock. At her side the German Shepherd growled dutifully, backed and slunk away, satisfied the strangers were no threat. Paula's faded cornflower eyes continued to monitor her visitors.

'I heard about you three.'

Her stare held a kind of resentment that bordered on anger. Now he was here after the long night, Nick discovered he had nothing to say. Instead, he was trying to calculate how old she was. About thirty. . .but middle-age had hit her early and hard. She said, 'I just knew you'd be back,' and smiled emptily. 'Still — at least you're not him.'

Nick said, 'Are you talking about my father?'

'Graham Hodge. I'd rather talk about him than *to* him, any day I would.' An infant's shriek lanced through the upper regions of the house; suddenly she was not unkind. 'Don't stand around out there. Shut the door behind you.' Just as suddenly, when they had crowded into the hall, she had turned into an army sergeant, bellowing, 'What's going on up there?' and striding away to the stairs. She went up them two at a time, hauling herself along on the bannister rail.

It was Eric who took the initiative. 'I'm tired and I want to sit down,' he said shortly. He pushed past Penny and Nick and his impetus dragged them behind him into the front room.

Penny was mildly surprised that the two downstairs reception rooms had not been knocked into one. This square room had not a stick of furniture in it; scatter cushions and grubby toys of an indefinably earlier period littered its bare floorboards. A large colour television was on very quietly, showing an imitation kitchen where two laughing strangers were drinking mugs of coffee and leafing through the morning newspapers. Camouflaged amongst a pile of cushions, a child of pre-school years was watching the television carefully, fearful of missing a moment of the commercial breaks, when they came. Eric seated himself down near the window and watched the screen precisely as the child was doing.

Penny and Nick sat down side by side. Their shoulders touched. Penny thought Nick would twitch himself away from this contact, but he did not. She looked around the room. The toys looked old because they were old. She felt sure they were second-hand. Sensible, really. She couldn't remember why it was sensible and then her mother's voice repeated to her, 'Toys are at their best when they're broken, because then the child has to use its imagination.' Funny that — she hadn't thought about Barbara for what seemed like weeks. . .

The small child ignored them as the dog had. Penny had almost grown accustomed to knocking on strange doors and sitting in strange rooms: perhaps this familiarity lay over all three of them like a light dusting of invisibility.

When Paula came into the room she brought with her a glowering toddler who closely resembled the child disguised among the cushions. The new child was an actor and he rehearsed his two lines with tiresome insistence. 'I no *want* to. I no *like* it,' he emoted, experimenting with improbable faces the while. Paula looked tired and spiteful now; she stood bouncing the boy savagely in the crook of her arm. They spoke loudly over his chant.

'Well?'

Penny and Nick got up. 'I. . .I understand you know my father,' Nick said with some force.

'Well?'

'We. . .we don't know where he is.'

'Well, *I* don't know where he is,' Paula said, amazed and angry.

'I no *like* it,' the child declaimed.

Nick said, 'You see, um, we're his children.'

'I'm an uncle,' Eric said dully.

Paula gave him a curious look and then called to Nick over the child's wails, 'If he's your father of course you're his children!' She jerked her head at Eric. 'What's this uncle business?'

'He's not our uncle,' Penny said, 'he's just helping us.'

'Helping you what — look for your dad?'

'Yes.'

'Where's your mum, then?'

'Away. They're not. . .they're separated.'

'Yes, I know. You be quiet!' This last was to the child, whom Paula plonked down beside — yes — its twin. The chanting stopped. The two siblings gave one another a blank stare and then gazed at the television. Paula transferred her attention to Eric. 'So just who are you, then?'

Still seated, Eric tried to keep his concentration on the TV set. 'I'm a friend. They wanted to find their dad. I do a bit of gardening.'

He was looking at the television as Paula glanced over at Nick and tapped the side of her head queryingly. Nick nodded confirmation, and her attitude to Eric lost its abrasive quality. 'What do you know about Graham Hodge, then? What's your name, anyway?'

'Eric. I don't know anything.' He was a police suspect resolutely sticking to his alibi. 'I do his garden. I don't know him at all.'

Paula folded her arms and took a couple of steps towards Nick and Penny.

'It's cost me blood to take today off. And money. I run a business. Now you two turn up, with your friend.'

'I'm sorry,' Nick said. 'We don't want to put you out. It's just...we came a long way to find out what was going on.'

'Done a bunk, has he?'

Penny recognized that it was Paula's toughness which gave her the middle-aged air she had, and not just her look of fatigue or her figure, which was melting into a pear-shape.

'Yes,' she answered, 'on Christmas Day.'

Naturally the statement was soaking with self-pity, although she had tried to sound as tough as Paula, who only responded, 'That sounds about right. Right for him.'

Why was she so bitter?

'Are you going to help us?' Nick asked, as pathetic as Penny.

'How much do you know about your dad?'

'Um...Well, I don't suppose we know anything. Not now.'

'You look like him,' Paula said quietly.

Penny said. 'We found out he's got a flat in London. There's two men who are looking for him. I think they wrecked his flat.'

'That doesn't surprise me,' said Paula, and it didn't. 'Do you know what I do here?'

'No,' said Penny, not understanding quite what the woman meant.

'I run my own car firm. I'm a single woman — these days I am — so I don't do mini-cabbing. I do parcels, packages...Sometimes it's just a letter. It's safer not to have men in your vehicle. But I used to drive your dad around. A bit. For a while...I met him through my ex. Ex-husband. I'm a fool to myself, I am.'

She had shut herself up for a moment. When she came

out of her reverie she said, 'You want to know about your dad, I'll show you.'

Every level of the old warehouse echoed with the sounds of the building trade and nowhere was it noisier than in the basement. Vincent's ears hurt and he could taste plaster dust. The fine particles caught at his throat and silted his nose. He coughed and it was like rubbing together two pieces of glasspaper. 'Leave it out a minute!' he shouted.

The man with the heavy-duty drill switched it off and raised his protective mask, which looked like a relic from the First World War. He called back across the room, 'How you doing? Taking a break?'

'What I'd like to take is a shower.'

Vincent looked vicious and the man said, 'Take it easy, son. Not my fault. These walls are like concrete.'

'Yeah? So why are they renewing them, then?'

'Damp reading.'

'It should've been done before I come.'

'You think I want to be here?'

'I should've been *told*.'

'Yeah? Made a difference, would it?'

Vincent made his lips thin. 'I like to be treated right.'

The man gave him a dismissive glance and lowered his mask. He re-powered the big drill.

Fighting back anger, Vincent ran his hand through his hair. It was thick with the pale dust and he could see that it had even infiltrated the fine red cracks in the hard skin of his hands. It made him more livid. Hard hands, hard life; soft hands. . .but what chance did he have of a soft life?

He let himself fondle the thought that somewhere out there was a man who owed him a sum of money it would take him nearly a month to earn in this uncongenial environment here. He took hold of the thought more tightly and found the hands he disliked so were beginning to pack his tool-case. Funny — he'd been so sure he'd come to terms with that loss...but he hadn't at all, not sweating away here like a common labourer...

He began to picture the row he would have with Tommy. You didn't treat a skilled worker like this. Next, he could see himself back in his blue suit, back on the streets, 'the main man' again.

He wondered in which places he should search for Graham, and started to hum 'Vincent', the Don McClean song.

She drove them all over London, hardly saying a word. Her car was a small estate car and she filled it with smoke from continuous cigarettes. The twins went with them in car seats Paula had buckled them into with impatient efficiency. The toddlers were situated on either side of Eric; it seemed they were car-babies, for they fell asleep almost as the engine started. Eric himself looked very tired.

Paula had correctly identified Nick as the team leader and he sat beside her in the front. For driving she wore white canvas shoes and above them he could see thick-stemmed blue veins in her ankles. He felt a deep aversion to her: practically a physical unease in her presence.

Penny sat alone on a drop-down seat in the rear of the car — where, presumably, the packages travelled. As the drive progressed she felt increasingly like a parcel herself; a drab and anonymous object with no will or volition of her own.

'I used to take him there,' Paula would say. Or, 'We went there a few times.' Her factual tones did not encourage comment as she pointed out three gambling clubs, a hotel with a casino, and even a greyhound stadium. As a professional driver, her knowledge of London was such that Penny rarely had any certainty as to exactly where they were. They would dart out of a side street into a major thoroughfare and Paula would say, 'There, we went there,' and Penny would lower her head to see and a great square, unlit neon dice would be there, suspended above a door, and Paula would drive on without pause until she slowed to wrench them out of the main stream of traffic and back into the byways of the city.

The practical, all but brutal way she drove told the tale as well as any words. Their father went to places where you gambled. Separated as they were in the car, Nick and Penny did not feel it was possible to communicate. What would one say, anyway? The sleeping twins swayed and lolled in their harnesses and on they went.

Remembering the seedy flat in Vauxhall, it was curious to emerge into the grandeur of Berkeley Square and hear Paula announce: 'The Clermont. We went there. Just the once. Too strong for him.' Her voice became brittle. 'He's a loser, your dad. Just my luck. No — not luck — something else. First my old man and then... Don't get me wrong. I don't hate all men. Just the ones I've met. Do you want to go on with this?'

Penny left it to Nick to answer. He couldn't. Sitting beside Paula, he was feeling a little car-sick, as far as he could recall the sensation. From what she said and the way she said it, it seemed likely that Paula and his father had been...had had an affair. This *woman*, whose figure was spreading like a pat of butter in the sun... Not a girl — a woman... This woman.

Compared to that, the rest of his father's secret life was insignificant at this moment.

Paula did not repeat her last abrupt question, so Nick and Penny did not know whether or not the tour of their father's haunts was continuing. The car took another corner, sharply.

It was at around this time that Graham woke up in a comfortable hotel room. He had not slept well for a year or so, and yet even though he had not been deep in sleep he was at first disoriented. The crispness of the bed-linen

136

alarmed him: he was in a hospital; something had happened... He was sweating, too. He sat up and the panic was lost in a wave of euphoria. He had come through! The bad run was over — he was back in charge of his own destiny and if he was sensible his chosen life was manageable, was ideal, was... *wonderful*. And he had two thousand pounds to prove it.

He was sweating only because he was boiling hot. He knew why he was hot, as well. He was in a small, inexpensive hotel amongst many in an enclave of Georgian streets just across the road from King's Cross. As with several of these hotels, this one advertised 'Full Central Heating' as though it was the ultimate in modern luxury, and what it promised was delivered in trumps.

How clever, how *sensible* he had been last night. Once again he had achieved his target winnings and walked away with not the remotest urge to go on and on, and afterwards he had resisted the vainglorious notion of putting up at the Great Northern Hotel right by the station. He was no profligate, he was a professional man with an irreproachable sense of responsibility... and two children. Suddenly he prickled all over with anxiety; his heart began to thud. He swung out of bed and put his head in his hands. How could he have done it? Was he mad? Who would leave their children by themselves as he had?

Graham got up and began to dress fast, to occupy himself. He was unaware that his clothes smelt of stale excitement and cigarette smoke from the One-Eyed Jack. Unwelcome thoughts spun round in his mind like a buzz-saw. Awful... *awful*...

Penny would tell her mother and then his secret existence would be blown into the open — and who except himself could understand how very rational and *possible* his new life was? Who, except Nick. His ally. His only friend. And that friend and ally would be taken from him for sure.

Despair battered him back on to the bed and he lay

there looking up at the ceiling until the screaming buzz-saw had shredded his capacity for any kind of rational thought.

'And there. We went there.'

The club was called the One-Eyed Jack and looked thoroughly cheap.

It seemed possible that Paula was punishing herself more than them, for they had long since ceased to react to the sights she was showing them. In as far as they were doing anything, they were waiting for the tour to end.

'Warmer now,' said Eric, of the weather, although from his tone it might have been a clue in a treasure hunt.

'Where next,' Paula mused. They drove away from the area, passing through Georgian side-streets crammed with small hotels.

In half an hour Graham felt fine again. He had not so much confronted the problem that had immobilized him, he had risen above it. The process was that you waited for the fears — whatever they might be — to wear themselves out a little and then you got positive with yourself: got the old fighting spirit back. He had refined the problem to its core element. The children would tell on him. OK, he would just have to bluff it through, in style, with irresistible presents for them and the manner that had so often worked with Nick. A mixture of rueful charm and the implicit attitude that his behaviour was, if not usual, at least acceptable. Treat them like adults in the way he spoke to them and like children with the things he gave to them...

It would be the same spurious confidence he would use when he checked out of this hotel; a man in stained clothing and without a single article of luggage, but with a man-of-the-world way with him which made any deficiencies quite immaterial because he willed it to be so.

As for his broader worries, they were soluble. He was a professional and it was time to rationalize, as though he was indeed running a one-man business. The London flat, regretfully, would have to go. He would have to start over again, setting himself cautious targets and meeting each one before he moved on to the next. Plan more carefully, monitor himself more closely and all would be well. The horror of the last few days need never return — and would never return.

'I am in charge of my own destiny,' he told himself, 'and with things running with me, there is nothing I can't achieve, with complete self-respect.'

The money he owed that disgusting Vincent was another matter. In fact the money he owed to several other people was another matter too... He couldn't waste any of his precious stake money that way. As a man of honour, of course the debts would be repaid eventually, but it would have to be when he could afford it.

Thinking about it, it was no bad thing that he would have to avoid Vincent and his kind...it had been a mistake to sink down to that level of gambling anyway...yes! Yes...that had been his fatal error! He should stick to what he knew! He had been mad to get into card-schools with that kind of man...mad.

Yet in the back of his mind he acknowledged that from such men as Vincent he had learnt some useful tricks...like the uses of that snooker hall when you were starting the day with minimal cash... And much less clearly he understood that a part of him had wanted to sink into that world: had desired it and got what it desired... He didn't want to think about that. It wouldn't happen again and that was all there was to it.

He'd better get busy before more unwanted thoughts crowded in.

Good. First thing: ring home. Confident apologies — that was first. Then a train and it would be as though he'd never gone away at all...almost... Wouldn't it?

139

Graham picked up the phone on the bedside table and got an outside line. But the phone at home in Cambridgeshire wasn't working and little pinpricks of fear began to run through him once more. He knew he hadn't paid the telephone bill, but surely... Will power... take *action*, gain...*momentum*.

In less than twenty minutes he had paid the hotel bill, bought his train ticket at King's Cross and had speed-walked into the station branch of W.H. Smith.

Presents. His train left in ten minutes. He'd be home in no time, but he had to have goodies to shower on Nick and Penny. It didn't matter how much he spent as long as the effect was stunning...overwhelming. But this little store was hardly Harrods... Will power; action; *momentum*. He gathered up an armful of boxed games and paid for them. Not very exciting, though — he'd have to create the effect through sheer quantity.

'Could you hold on to these for a moment?' he asked the girl at the till. 'I feel like spending today!'

Books. Plenty of those here. The girl on the till had looked friendly, he thought, impressed by his charm. He could easily charm away the doubts of his children — no problem. Just keep switched *on* here, he told himself. Books for Nick. Easy. A paperback advising which personal computer would suit your needs...that'd get Nick going. Naturally he'd assume he'd be getting a PC soon — and naturally when finances were back to strength he would get one, so it wasn't really a deception... A couple of thrillers — really adult ones — that'd impress him too. *The Guinness Book of Records* — he'd not got that, Graham knew... Ah — and a leather Filofax — brilliant!

Now for Penny...and suddenly the momentum collapsed. How could he be certain of winning her over with gifts when he had no idea what she liked — or what any girl of her age liked? Distracted, it came to him, really I need wrapping paper for everything I buy — this is *impossible*! He started to hate Penny. He'd only got a couple of minutes — and it was as if she was here at his elbow deliberately trying to sabotage him.

Romantic fiction. But perhaps she had only one favourite author? Or pet hates. . . Would *she* like a Filofax? Something on fashion? So far he knew that her mother would approve of none of these things, but that was of no consequence; it was Penny he had to please. How? *Quick.* Fountain pen. Only plastic ones here: too cheap. OK — buy two. They need ink cartridges — get lots. Books books books — wrapping paper — he was being driven mad here. Fine. Two big rolls of wrapping paper. Hard to carry this lot. . .*you can do it.* Historical romantic fiction. Take a chance — take five at random. . .

Close to dementia now, he reached for a shiny hardback about the Royal Family and dropped every single article he was clutching.

He scrabbled about on the floor, gathering the things. The girl on the till was looking at him strangely.

'*Help me,*' he snarled at her, crouching like a werewolf among the litter of his gifts.

A few minutes later, toting four bulging carrier bags, he watched his train sliding out of the station without him.

Graham's rage knew no bounds. He didn't care that another train left in only half an hour: his brilliant plan had been destroyed. It was *unfair.* He had only been thinking of his children.

He looked at his watch. Half an hour to kill. . . Hello — the One-Eyed Jack would just be opening. . . He wouldn't gamble, but he could take a quick peek in there, to feel the ambience and savour his success of the night before. . .

He went out of the station with his luggage of bribes, walked rapidly to the club and lost two thousand pounds in fifteen minutes.

He boarded the Cambridge train with a pale face and hugely staring eyes.

CHAPTER 10

PAULA'S DEDICATION to self-punishment, if that was what it was, took a vast bite out of the day. When they paused outside a run-down snooker hall Penny and Nick began to sense that the end was in sight. She must be scraping the bottom of the barrel here.

'Here... Sometimes I'd wait for him outside this place,' Paula said wearily. Even her driving had become more sluggish in the last hour.

The hall had the chalet-look of a certain kind of Methodist chapel and might once have been one. Nick came to life a little. 'He plays snooker too? I didn't know that.'

His interest in such a trivial detail irked Penny and she too began to emerge from the dull trance which had held them. 'We don't have to go on with this, do we? I think we've got the message. Unless there's something else you want to tell us.'

Paula's shoulders sagged. 'No. That's the whole story, give or take a few other joints. You get it, do you?'

'Yes, thank you,' Nick said politely. For a second he was a keen-eyed policeman: 'Unless there's something else you want to tell us, that is.'

The suspicious note was not lost on Paula. 'There's nothing more you need to know,' she said sharply, and a spitting anger erupted. 'All this...this stuff I've been showing you — that's what your dad likes to do. That's what he needs to do. He's a sick man — ill.'

'You're a doctor, are you, as well as a driver,' Nick said rudely.

She gave him a long stare. 'Where d'you want to go? I'll give you a lift.'

'No, thank you very much,' Nick said, rather overdoing the politeness this time.

Penny said, 'Well...'

'No. We've found out all we need to know. There's no point in putting her to any more trouble.'

'Fine,' Paula said. 'Out you get, then.'

Eric spoke. 'Excuse me...'

'Oh, you're still here, are you?'

'Yes. I know it's not good manners to say it, but we haven't got any money. I'm quite old, so I should have some money, but I haven't. That makes me feel uncomfortable with myself. I was doing some breathing just now. Actually I've just remembered. I was doing it backwards.'

There was a small silence while Paula tried to find her way amongst all this. She turned to Nick. 'Broke, are you? Must run in the family.' She rooted about in her handbag, down by her feet. 'There's a fiver. Enough?'

'We can't,' said Nick. All at once he was very troubled.

'Why not? This is nothing. Your dad owes me five hundred.'

There was another little silence.

'Then thanks,' said Penny. 'Thanks very much. Take it, Nick. Just take it.'

Nick took the note. 'Um...' He was increasingly upset.

'Out you get,' said Paula. 'I've got troubles of my own.' She frowned away the temptation to be nicer to him.

The twins slumbered on in slack-jawed serenity as the three travellers left the car. Perhaps they didn't sleep at night, Penny thought. No wonder their mother seemed so frazzled.

Paula wound down her window. Now, as she was parting from them, her defences slipped and emotion came into her voice. 'Listen. You did get it, didn't you? Your dad needs help. He needs shooting too, but he needs help.'

Penny was nearest and she bent down to the window. 'Yes. I think we got it. Thank you.'

Paula would not meet her gaze. 'I don't want to see you

again.' She pulled out into the traffic with a short protest from the tyres.

'Wow,' said Nick.

'Yeah. Wow,' said Penny.

Graham sat on the train in a state of shock and pain one might associate with multiple deaths in the family, although his family was the last thing on his mind at present.

His lips moved in a repetitious pattern. He was saying, 'How could I have *done* it? *How*?' much as Paula's toddler had been stuck on, 'I no want to, I no like it.' In half an hour or so he would revert to the plain 'no no no no no' he used when he felt life was against him.

As he entered the snooker hall, Nick was functioning on auto-pilot. Now he had learnt the truth about his father and it all fitted and yet he didn't know what to think about it...he didn't yet have an attitude to it. It was like being told you had cancer, maybe — at first the idea that you might die was so foreign that you didn't have the proper response...if there was a proper response. Somewhere in his confusion he understood that his search for Graham had gone as far as it could and he had wandered in here partly because it didn't tie in with the rest of the story and partly because he didn't know how to abandon his quest at just a moment's notice.

He had no firm idea what he intended to do in the old hall, but once in he found it gratifying that no one questioned his right to be here...he must look eighteen at least. But then, it was exceedingly murky in here, so it could be that the man behind the little bar at one side of the room could not see him very well. And there was a sign above the bar saying 'No Alcohol Served', so age might not be a bar to entry in any case.

The chapel or church effect was enhanced by the layout

of the hall. There was a central aisle between the twenty low snooker tables which stretched away from him, rock-solid on their heavy, carved mahogany legs. There were dead areas of deep shadow where the tables were not being played on, but the ones in current use were lit and on these the light itself was reminiscent of a church service, for the rectangular shades hanging close to the tables cast down on to the green baize a warm yellow glow like that of candles.

Nick's troubles receded; he was captivated by the quiet drama of the arena. As his eyes became accustomed to the dimness he saw that the seating all along the walls was actually a series of old church pews. They might have been chosen because they had been cheap and took up little space.

Then he realized that several of the pews were occupied. Sitting around the hall was an assembly of men who, however disparately they were dressed, shared one common attribute: they were old.

Some of the old men were very old indeed and they seemed to sit even more still and even more silent than their companions, as if their remaining energies were devoted solely to living as long as possible. Only their eyes moved, and there was an un-nervingly watchful quality to them. Some of the men were looking at him and it made him ridiculously unsure of himself.

He looked straight ahead of him and strolled further into the hall. A black youth in a leather bomber jacket was on his own at a table close by, potting blue, pink and black, the last of the colours. Because he was nearer in age to Nick than the others here, Nick took up station by him, leaning back with his hands resting on one of the tables not in use. He tried to look cool and in his own imagination succeeded.

The bomber-jacketed youth potted the blue and left himself nicely on the pink. Coming round the table to play it, he saw Nick.

145

'Yo.'

'Hi,' Nick muttered.

'You play this game?'

'Um...yuh.'

'Yeah?' The youth grinned widely. 'Well, rack 'em up, boy.' He took out a pack of cigarettes and lit one with a lighter in the shape of an automatic pistol. 'Don't stand around, man. Rack the balls. I ain't going to eat you.'

'I, er, I haven't got any money.'

'I paid for the lights — you don't need none. Get it on.'

Outside, Eric was happy again. He had a sandwich. There had been two in the packet and Penny was just finishing hers. They stood near the door of the snooker hall, waiting for Nick.

Penny yawned. She was suddenly so tired that the pavement appeared to be shifting under her feet and she swayed against Eric.

'All right, Penny?'

She nodded and it felt that the action took a long time. All the impetus had left her as the information about their father had seeped in. Paula's method of telling them may have been lengthy, but it had been effective — a journey around the evidence, there in all three dimensions and beyond challenge, and *shocking*...and...why wasn't she more concerned? Her father was a no-good waster who cared more about gambling than about his family and it seemed quite normal to Penny. Perhaps because her mother had somehow programmed her to expect the worst of Graham. But, poor Nick. His world must be in ruins. He and Penny had barely spoken since leaving the car, so she could only guess at the state of his emotions. What must he be feeling...?

She watched Eric pop the last of the sandwich into his mouth. He licked his fingers, giving each one individual attention, as he always did. Penny felt restless. They should move on now. Get back to the country, she supposed...that would be the best thing to do. She

146

couldn't see what Nick hoped to accomplish in the snooker hall. It might be that he simply wanted to get away from them — from her — for a while. Though they had been getting on really quite well, all things considered. But really they should be going now.

'Eric.'

'Yes, Penny?'

She was about to ask him to go into the hall and get Nick out, but on impulse asked instead, 'What do you think about what that woman showed us?'

'It looks as though your dad has been gambling,' Eric said seriously, 'and he's got himself into some bother.'

Penny sighed. 'Yes — but what do you think about it? I mean — have you ever gambled, Eric?'

He thought. 'I don't know. I suppose I must have...'

Hopeless. As ever. 'Could you go in there a minute, and get Nick, do you think?'

'All right. Would you be all right here?'

'If you weren't too long.'

'Right you are. Now?'

'In a minute. I don't want to nag him. He's very upset.'

Nick was not sure he had ever experienced such intense excitement. His hands were shaking as he chalked the cue. To be standing here in this temple to snooker, playing a street-wise black guy in a bomber jacket, was as close to heaven as he could imagine. On a full-size table, too! And his first shot had drawn appreciation from Bomber Jacket — he had rapped the butt of his cue on the floor when the white ball came back past the baulk line, almost to the cushion, perfectly safe.

Now Bomber Jacket played into the pack of reds, softly, but not softly enough, for the pack rippled open and there was a red on into the centre pocket. Nick studied the shot with a worrying lack of inner calm.

As he bent down to the table a figure came out of the darkness into his eyeline. It was one of the old men. Another came up behind the first. He had some kind of

147

chest problem and Nick could hear a bubbling noise as he drew in breath. A black guy, a full-size table, and now an audience... Nick steeled himself and played and the target red went into the pocket without touching the sides.

Penny said, 'Go on, then, Eric. We can't hang about here all day.'

'Go and get him, you mean?'

'Yes. Please.'

'And you'll be all right?'

'Tell him we've got to be moving on.'

'All right, Penny.' Eric lumbered into the snooker hall.

To her dismay, as soon as she was left alone, Penny started to cry. She had no idea why: it came as a total surprise to her and it hurt her throat and stomach muscles because it seemed important to hold on to the tears and not let them show.

Bomber Jacket was building a break. His positional play was not as good as Nick's, as Nick thought, but he had a good eye and was capable of making some marvellous long pots. Nick had been relieved when his own break had come to a premature end, because the pressure was getting to him. At this moment he was not watching the black teenager in play, for he was witnessing the reason why his father had come here every now and then.

Over and above simple survival these old men had an interest in life. Whenever a shot was played sums of money changed hands surreptitiously. Ancient hands passed over pound coins and five-pound notes, without a word spoken. As the next shot was considered, bets were agreed incredibly quickly by a sign language that involved laying a certain number of fingers on one's opposing forearm — but the tic-tac speed of it made it impossible to comprehend fully how the system worked. What was clear was that it was a point of honour not to react in any way to one's success or failure. If it reminded Nick of anything, it was of a geriatric stock exchange.

Eric's face appeared between two of the old men. He

was grimacing and gesturing for Nick to come to him. The old men became aware of his presence and paused in their immediate transaction.

'Nick!' Eric hissed urgently. His presence was a major embarrassment to Nick, who would have liked to ignore him. It was not possible.

'Penny wants you!'

'In a minute, Eric. I'm busy.'

'But she wants you!'

'I said, in a minute!'

The old men were getting agitated. Bomber Jacket looked up from the snooker table. 'Could I have a bit of hush here?'

'Go and sit down, Eric. Just for a minute.'

'But Penny —'

Nick lost his temper. 'Sit down and shut up — all right?'

Penny found it was less uncomfortable if she moved about a bit. She walked up and down the pavement quite rapidly, in an uncoordinated way, slightly bent over. When the volcanic inner sobs quieted she took a few deep breaths.

She was standing outside an undertaker's establishment. It had a shop window, at either side of which dark curtains were tied back to allow a discreet display of some of the items you could buy here. Etched into a black tombstone was the inducement: 'A DESIGN OF YOUR CHOICE CAN BE SANDBLASTED ON TO THIS MEMORIAL.'

In conjunction with the glass of the window, the black slab created a mirror in which Penny could see herself: a short, dismal figure which had been superimposed on the headstone as a possible design of choice. Another figure loomed at her shoulder in the dark mirror; a narrow figure in a dark suit, a figure that seemed to grow taller as it came closer to her. She froze as it leant down to speak into her ear.

'Hello, sweetheart.'

It was one of the men from her father's flat and there was a ringing note of triumph in his whisper. She tried

149

to turn but a vice-like hand squeezed hard on the nape of her neck.

'I don't want you going anywhere till we've had a talk. Now you stand quite still or I'll punch you straight through that window. Are you reading me?'

Her knees began to quiver. 'Yes.'

'Your dad... Is Graham Hodge your dad?'

There seemed no point in denying it. 'Yes.'

'Yes? Your dad — he's not watching the snooker, is he?' The hand tightened painfully on her neck. 'Is he?'

'No.'

'No, that's right, because I looked in and there's just your brother there and that other fella. Are you expecting your dad? Waiting for him, are you?'

'No.'

'I'm going to hurt you if you tell me fibs.'

'I'm not.'

'I might hurt you anyway. Where is he?'

'I don't know. Nobody knows.'

'And nobody cares, sweetheart. No one except me. But I care a lot.'

She could feel the warmth of his breath in her ear. It was disgustingly intimate. 'Leave me alone!'

'Sorry, sweetie.' His fingers crept up to the base of her skull and dug in until she had a headache. 'I can't leave you alone. I need you. I need you to tell me things. Where do you live?'

'I live with my mother. They're divorced.'

'Is that right?' He was slowly pressing her face into the glass.

'Mmn.' Couldn't anybody see what was going on? How could one feel so alone in a public place?

'So where does your dad live?'

'You know where.' Her voice was muffled and she felt the panic of claustrophobia. 'That's where he lives.'

'Oh, honey. I don't believe you.'

The pressure grew on her cheekbone. She was going to

go through the glass. But she couldn't tell him. She *mustn't*.
'Please. . .'

'Just give me an address where I can find him. Where does he work?'

She screamed. Her throat seemed to tear with the sound. In letting her go the man bounced her face hard against the window. Now they were facing each other and she was still screaming, looking straight at him.

Vincent looked at the girl with horror. He wanted to hit her to keep her quiet, but instead tore at her shoulder-bag. 'Give me that!'

She went on screaming. He tore at the bag until the strap broke. The bag fell to the ground and they both bent to pick it up. The screaming went on as some kind of disembodied sound-track. Vincent pushed Penny over and snatched up the bag and ran off, feeling as foolish and as furious as he had ever felt in his life.

Absorbed in the angles required to get out of a snooker, Nick was only dimly aware of the screaming from down the street. Eric heard it, but to him it sounded not at all like Penny, more like the frenetic despair of a much older person who'd had too much to drink. He'd heard a few of those over the years. Nevertheless, this wild woman might be distressing Penny or even harassing her in some way, so with a polite 'excuse me' to the old men with whom he was sharing a church pew, he stood up and walked out into the daylight.

Nick duly got out of the snooker, and was conscious that money was changing hands again, and yet the euphoria was fading. He was not likely to be back on the table for some time, since the white ball had not finished kindly for him. But he just had to stay here until he had established his credentials as a genuine player of the game. He had to show them. It was a matter of honour and self-respect now.

He felt a bit guilty about Penny and Eric, but it couldn't be helped, not now he had gone this far. . . He deliberately kept from glancing over at where Eric was sitting.

But Eric was at his side. 'Nick! Something's happened to Penny! There's a crowd and everything! The police'll be here soon!'

It was amazing how his anxiety for his sister over-rode any other consideration. 'Hold this. I've got to go.' He pressed the snooker cue into the hand of a rock-faced old man wearing an incongruous mohair suit, and ran out of the hall.

It was hardly a crowd. Three elderly women had gathered outside the undertaker's some thirty metres down the road, where Penny was testing her ability to walk. She had hurt her ankle. Nick ran to her. 'What happened?'

'Some dirty brute knocked her down and snatched her bag,' one of the women said.

'I've sent my Jack for the police,' said another.

Eric was with them now. 'What happened, Penny?'

'Some dirty brute,' the first woman started, with satisfaction. Nick cut her off.

'I'm family. She's my sister. I'll handle this.'

'Oh.' The women were disappointed.

Penny's head was down. Nick put an arm round her. 'Are you all right?'

She spoke in such a low voice that even he could only just hear her. 'It was one of the men who wrecked the flat. He took my bag.'

'Ah.' The guilt he had felt in the snooker hall was nothing to that he felt now. 'Look — can you walk?' She lifted her head, and nodded. He could see a red mark on her cheekbone. 'Come on, then.'

'What about the police?' the second woman asked.

'Oh...um...it doesn't matter. It's family. It's OK.'

Eric took Penny by the elbow. 'I'm sorry, Penny.'

'It doesn't matter.' There was a tube station in sight across the road and Nick took them in that general direction.

'Talk about gratitude,' they heard the second woman say.

152

When they were some distance away from the undertaker's shop they waited for an opportunity to cross the road.

'Nick, we've got to get back to Cambridge,' Penny said. 'I know. Probably that's where Dad is now. Well — maybe. We should get back, anyway.'

'Yes. Because my diary was in my bag.'

'Sorry?'

'It's got your address in it. His address.'

He looked at her with horror. 'Oh *no*.'

They sat in a row on the bench-seating of the underground train, Eric and Nick on either side of Penny in a belated gesture of protection. There was no other option open to them but to get to the money in the charities jar at Barbara's house. When they got back to Cambridgeshire they could warn Graham, if he was there, that there could be trouble heading his way... Unless it had reached him already. The thought had crossed Nick's mind that if his father was not there, they themselves might again encounter the scary men from the flat. He was courageous enough not to share this thought with the others.

Though still in a minor state of shock, Penny was very aware that the normal rules seemed to apply for people in a hurry. The train spent long moments stationary in the tunnel, and would then travel on only slowly, as if it was the last in a traffic jam of underground trains. She was aware too, that Eric kept looking at her. The red mark on her cheek was hot and it seemed his stare was causing the heat, like a laser beam focused on its target. At last she had to look at him.

'Yes, Eric? Something on your mind?'

'No one should hurt a kiddy,' he said: it was the eleventh Commandment or possibly even the first.

'Fine,' she said shortly. 'I'm glad we've got that sorted out. Now could you look somewhere else?'

With an obvious effort Eric looked away. He began to

breathe in through his nose and whoosh the air out through pursed lips.

'Now what are you doing?'

'I'm doing my breathing. I remembered — I had it round the wrong way. You do the nose first. I was silly.'

Later in the journey she knew he was again looking at her. When his gaze was on Penny he suspended the breathing exercise and when he looked away again he went back to it with renewed vigour.

It was only a matter of days since Penny had left her home and yet, walking quickly down the street to it now, she felt like a returned time-traveller. These three-up, two-down terraced cottages had existed, completely unaltered, for a short space of real time while she had journeyed through light years of experience. It was like coming back as a grown-up; the house even looked smaller.

'Hang on. Key.'

Eric and Nick waited with an assumption of nonchalance, looking up and down the road as she lifted the broken flowerpot by the drain. She felt a burden of worry lifted: the two keys were there, as they always had been since she could remember. Some things at least didn't change. When she fumbled to open the front door she realized how numb her fingers were. She had become used to feeling cold.

'Come on. In we go. I wish we had time for a bath.'

'We haven't,' said Nick brusquely.

'I know, I only said...'

Let it go. She was home. She led the way through to the kitchen, passing through the series of subtly changing smells that her body always remembered even if she didn't. Unoccupied for a period, the house had accustomed itself to silence and one didn't like to make too much noise. Perhaps ghosts felt this... She felt a bit like a ghost herself. It would be nice to see her room... But — ah — the kitchen

154

would do! The scrubbed wooden table, the hanging brass saucepans, the numerous spice racks on the walls: glorious, friendly chaos. And dominating the clutter, the badly-split Welsh dresser bought for a song when Mummy was feeling flush... And on the dresser, the largest spaghetti jar in the world.

'Can I have a glass of water?' Eric asked courteously.

'No!'

'What?' asked Nick.

'Why?' asked Eric.

'She couldn't have...'

The money-level in the jar had subsided. Instead of a treasure trove of piled silver there was only a muddy residue of copper coins.

Nick came to her side and picked up the jar. With ease.

'We're done,' he said.

CHAPTER 11

'HOW COULD she have been so selfish?'

The coins stood in rounded towers on the flat plains of the kitchen table, arrayed for ease of counting.

Nick pushed out a finger and one of the towers collapsed.

'Selfish!' he repeated fiercely.

'They needed it for the trip,' Penny defended. 'We don't have much money. We're not like...' but of course she couldn't say 'not like you' any more.

Eric took a dainty sip of his water. 'I'm fed up with talking about money. It's all we ever talk about. There are other things in life. I'm sorry, but that's what I think.' He was pleased with himself.

'You've got the brains of a lobotomized baboon, Eric,' Nick said. 'We've got to get home and we've got a total of seven pounds to do it with. If you've got any constructive ideas we'd be happy to hear them. Amazed — but happy. Otherwise, shut up.'

'Sorry, Nick,' Eric said humbly.

Nick warmed to his own sense of superiority. 'What do you think money is — just stuff to exchange for food? Is that what you think? It isn't. The world runs on money — just like a car runs on petrol.'

Idly, he fingered a twopenny piece. Penny imagined he was contemplating the brilliance of what he had just said. When he spoke again, reflectively, she was quite unprepared for his line of thought.

'Our mother's got a car, hasn't she, Pen...?'

'Sorry?'

'It'd be a question of petrol...'

Now she could feel his excitement as a tangible presence

in the room. 'No! Absolutely not! You can't!'

'Well, the thing is you see, I actually can — can drive a car, that is.'

'You can't — we can't!'

'You've seen me drive, haven't you, Eric?'

'Well...'

'Look, Penny — it's not a big car. Dad's was much bigger and I could manage that.'

'But this is London, Nick — not a country road.'

'I've been in traffic.'

'Not like London.'

'It's an automatic! Automatic gears, I remember!'

She wished he hadn't. 'That doesn't make it any easier,' she said lamely.

'Of course it does — that's what they're for — that's why she's got them!'

Eric said, 'It's against the law to drive if you're too young and you haven't got a licence.'

Nick pretended astonishment. 'Eric — that's incredible — have you been reading again?'

'You shouldn't break the law. What if a police car...' Eric got up, deeply perturbed. Penny saw that he was on to something here.

'That's right, Nick. OK — you know how to drive, but honestly, you don't look old enough. We wouldn't get two miles.'

'Have you got any sunglasses in the house?'

'Oh, come off it!'

'I'd look old enough, then.'

'You'd look blind. And it's not going to be light enough for dark glasses.' But almost against her will she was beginning to get used to the idea.

'A hat. That'd do it,' Nick said.

'A hat?'

Graham walked the streets of Cambridge with his hands

in his pockets. He would start hitching a lift when he got to a point where cars would be more likely to be going his way. He kept his eyes on a spot on the pavement just in front of his feet. Life was pointless and — worse — annoying. It was inconvenient and — worse — painful. Every now and then he twitched as he walked, fighting a compulsion to shout and thresh about. He wanted to hurt whatever it was that was hurting him, and there was nothing here to hurt.

He plodded on. He'd have to have a story ready for why he didn't have any money...but the children might be impressed by how he had — for them — walked all the way back from Cambridge... That's what he'd tell them, even if he got a lift right to the door. 'I walked all the way here. For you. I came as soon as I could.'

It might be necessary to tell Nick he'd lost his job. Now might be the moment, when he needed sympathy... It would be a confession hurtful to his pride but if it had to be made, it had to be made. 'I went down to London in good faith — at Christmas — worked my guts out for them and they sacked me!'

But once he admitted he was out of work he'd changed the whole ball-game. He'd have to play that one by ear. Use it as a trump card if the going got really rough... 'I didn't want to worry you, but...'

The hat was grey felt and would have been commonplace in a black and white gangster movie. It was Barbara's; maybe that was why Penny had an urge to snigger every time she looked at Nick. Her state of nervousness had made her quite light-headed: she had giggled earlier while she was searching out the car keys, even as she was thinking, 'I should just pretend there isn't a spare set, or pretend I can't find them.'

Nick had already forgotten about the hat he wore. He was having problems opening the door of the little white car. It caused him to doubt his ability to drive the thing once they got in. He must look like a car thief, with the time he was taking...

Eric still stood by the door of the house, out of sight from most of the street. Was he going to make a dash for the car when it had started, Penny wondered? As if he were someone the press or the police mustn't see?

'Ah!' The door opened. 'You go in the back, Pen. I want Eric beside me. Looks better. You read the map.'

It was a two-door car so Penny squeezed in past the angled front seat. She rather tumbled in, since she was holding a carrier bag containing all the coins from the spaghetti jar. The money seemed disproportionately heavy for its value.

Nick called quietly, 'Come on, Eric.'

Penny could just make out Eric's soft answer: 'We mustn't.'

'Come *on*.'

'You don't know what you're doing.'

Nick shouted, 'Come here!' and Eric came like a pop-star escaping a mob, as Penny had thought he would. She giggled again. The car crouched closer to the road as he lowered himself into the passenger seat.

'This is dreadful.'

'Shut up, Eric.' Nick's hands were slippery as he fitted the key in the ignition. He turned the key and the car jolted backwards sharply and stopped.

'Nick!'

'Shut *up*, Penny.' He did what he should have done on first getting into the car, checking the rear-view mirror; adjusting his seat. The process calmed him a little.

Penny asked, 'Are you OK?' and the tension returned.

'Yes — fine!' he snapped. He looked at the automatic gear-stick. It had three positions: Drive, Park and R, for reverse, and that was what he was in. Well, that should be simple enough. And he mustn't forget to let the handbrake off, as he so often had on Dad's car...

159

'Have you changed your mind?' Eric said, with hope. 'Shall we get out?'

'No. You look in the dash and get out the road maps. Give them to Penny. We're looking for the A1 from here, I think.'

They sat in the stationary car for a good twenty minutes, while Penny tried to plan their route out of London.

Eric glanced around the street in fear and guilt, waiting for discovery by a passer-by and then thereafter a variety of consequences, all unpleasant. Only one person came down the road, a young mother with a push-chair around which an opaque weatherproof covering was stretched like cling-film, so that the chair's occupant could be seen only as a blob. The young woman was in a hurry and did not look at the car: she wanted to get her baby home before the lowering clouds delivered yet more rain. Although it was only mid-afternoon, the day was darkening as the travellers sat there.

Nick used the time to rehearse in his mind the procedures needed to drive this particular car. He remembered now that it was standard practice to leave cars in reverse, for safety reasons...there was no clutch to work, of course... He'd check the petrol gauge when he started up the engine again... The lights seemed easy enough, and the indicators, if he remembered to use them — that was another of his failings as a driver... To move off you must just put the shift in drive and press down on the accelerator...

They were ready. 'Golders Green. I can get us there and we'll get on to the North Circular,' said Penny, with a confidence she didn't feel. The maps were old enough to be out of date and the job of navigation was new to her.

Nick cleared his throat as if about to make a speech in front of a big audience and started the car. He waited for the petrol gauge to settle itself. It looked as if there was less than a quarter of a tank and without telling the others he made a mental note that at some point they would have to stop for petrol. No need to worry them with that yet, though. . . He let off the handbrake. It looked as if he had room to nose out without any reversing. His foot pressed gently on the accelerator and they were under way. He turned the wheel and could feel that there was no power steering.

'Nick!' Penny shrieked again. A van swerved past them in a snarl of sound, playing an angry tune on its horn: Nick had forgotten to look.

'Nick! You're going to get us killed!'

'Why don't you stop thinking about yourself and think about Dad for a change?' Yes—attack, the best form of defence. 'What I need here is a little encouragement— a little support! You're making me nervous.'

Penny couldn't believe it. 'We're making *you* nervous?'

'Just concentrate on your job. Where do we go at the top of the road?'

'Left. Then right on to the High Street.'

'Good.' He echoed the black youth in the snooker hall. 'Now can I have some hush in here?'

'All right, Nick,' said Eric, who hadn't spoken.

The car pulled out into the road, smoothly, and Nick pressed cautiously on the accelerator.

Graham sat high above the road in the cab of a lorry. If you looked at it one way, his luck was in again, because it was a very superior lorry that had stopped for him. German-made, the driver had told him, and they had had a comfortable conversation about how wonderful German manufacturing was and how Britain may have won the Second World War but the Germans had won the peace hands down.

'You look all in, if you don't mind my saying so,' the driver was saying.

'Do I?' Graham said, surprised. He was feeling better again. 'Well, I had a hectic time in London. I've been working incredibly hard just recently and I realized I'd been neglecting the children rather.' After a pause he added, 'They've got a nanny. She's very good, but I'm afraid they saw a lot more of her than they did of me over Christmas. So — I dashed up to London and gathered up all the presents I could think of. Spent the lot.' He laughed convincingly. 'I was in such a hurry I left my credit cards at home! It was lucky I had the train ticket — the rest went on the kids.'

The driver looked at him curiously. 'Yes? What you get them?'

'Oh the lot. Everything I could lay my hands on!'

'Yes?' Again he glanced at his passenger.

'Yes. Here.'

But there were no carrier bags at his feet. He had left them on the train.

'Oh *no*!'

The driver looked away, disconcerted. It looked as though the shabby man was going to cry.

Eric was sweating so hard his face looked as if it was streaming with tears. Penny knew just how he felt: the High Street had been a nightmare.

Nick's shoulders were up round his ears and he was gripping the steering wheel too hard. He knew it, and he couldn't do anything about it. His confidence was in tatters. The High Street was entered at a junction on a slight hill and he had stalled, nearly rolling back into the car behind him. His judgement of distance in traffic had been wayward and he was finding it hard even to steer a straight line. It was like learning all over again. He didn't seem to be able to synchronize his speed with the rest of the traffic and the car jerked along as if there was something wrong with the clutch, sometimes too fast and sometimes too slow.

Penny had gradually sunk down in her seat as people do during the showing of a well-made horror film.

'You're much too close to the kerb, Nick,' she said, as calmly as she could.

'I know. I can't help it.' The instinct was to take up as little space on the road as possible. They were out of the crowded High Street now and yet he still didn't feel at all settled.

Unwittingly, Penny's method of navigation did not help. It was founded on the theory that the more main roads they avoided, the better, and it was not a confidence builder for Nick. Given the opportunity, the anxious learner driver would travel everywhere in a series of left turns, without once having to move across oncoming traffic; as it was he was continually having to make turns to the right and it was stretching his nerve to its limits.

More traffic lights ahead. No hill-start this time; good.

'To the right, here, Nick.'

'Again? We're going round in circles, aren't we?'

'No. I've got it all worked out. Just get in the right-hand lane, will you?'

'I'm sure we could go left here.'

'Just get in the lane!' There was panic in her voice and Nick reacted to it, wrenching the car into the centre of the road.

There was a by now familiar accompaniment to the manoeuvre: elephantine trumpetings of rage sounded from a car horn behind them.

'Oh, Nick...'

'Don't "Oh Nick" me. That was your fault!'

'The lights!'

They had already gone from amber to red. Nick stepped on the brakes and the car skewed to a stop. Luckily it had pulled itself towards the pavement and there was plenty of room for the high-cabined pick-up truck to take up station alongside. Its driver was a ginger-haired man in a red check lumber shirt; he had his window wound down in masculine defiance of the elements. All that was missing was a beer can in his hand, from a six-pack. A superior in-car stereo system relayed a syrupy Christmas message from a country and western singer — something about there being a new little man in the world today. 'He'll be someone to turn to, when your spirits are low, and he'll take your hand when it's your time to go. . .'

Nick knew that the driver was looking down into the car and kept his head at an angle, hoping the hat would obscure his face. The traffic lights stayed at red forever. As they changed, the man in the pick-up truck finally said his piece, with uncanny accuracy.

'I'd turn around if I was you. Your L-plates fell off.' As the open truck surged away on a wave of country and western heartache the man bawled, 'Women drivers!'

Nick stalled again. He covered his confusion with, 'Where next? Come on!'

'We get on the North Circular up round Barnet. I told you.'

'I don't think you know where we are at all.' He re-started the car and they jerked off again. Women drivers. . . He looked like a woman, did he. That was all he needed. He wanted to be angry, but he was only upset. He turned into the next street and ran straight into a pile of bulging black rubbish bags in the gutter.

They were all thrown forward by the impact. Nick stayed where he was, head in his hands on the wheel.

'Nick! Are you all right?'

He mumbled. 'I can't do it. I can't do it.'

'It doesn't matter. Really. We can leave the car here and get back to the house. You tried. It doesn't matter.'

He took off the offending hat and crumpled it. 'Doesn't matter? Doesn't matter? Of course it matters!' He sounded hysterical.

'You did your best,' Penny soothed.

'And I haven't finished yet. You believe me. I'll get us there. Don't you worry. All right — I'm not much of a driver — but I'll get us there!'

'You'll get us killed — that's what you'll do!'

164

'I don't—'

Eric had something to say. 'Put your hat on!'

No one could panic quite like Eric and Nick was jamming the hat back on his head even as he asked, 'Why?'

'They're all looking at us!'

It was true. The occupants of passing cars gazed at them with the frank curiosity of those who had never been in a collision with a pile of refuse sacks.

Once again Nick had to re-start the car. When he tried to reverse from the sacks they held on to the front bumper.

'Give me a hand. Quickly.'

He got out of the car. His desire was to get away before any pedestrians turned up to help. Penny and Eric followed more slowly.

Two of the bags had become wedged under the bumper. He pulled at the black plastic, ripping the swollen sacks, which gave off a sweet rotting smell as they surrendered their contents. The serrations on the rim of an opened can of tomatoes sliced a cut into the flesh between his forefinger and thumb. He ignored the blood mingling with the thin tomato juice and kicked away the first bag. Penny arrived in time to at least look as if she was helping him drag away the second sack.

Eric did not arrive at all. After clambering out he stood stock still, in Nick's way as he hurried back to the driver's door. Penny came after Nick instead of going to the passenger side.

'Your hand...'

'It doesn't matter. I can't even feel it. All that matters is that we get home.'

'It could be infected.'

'I don't care. Get out of the way, Eric.'

Eric said, 'Give me the hat, Nick.'

'Get in the car, Eric.'

'Give me the hat.'

'We can't stand around here.'

'I'm going to drive. Give me the hat.'

'What!'

Eric reached out and plucked the hat from Nick's head and put it on his own. 'Get in the back, Penny.'

He looked sillier even than Nick, in the woman's felt hat.

'You're crazy, Eric. You have to know how to drive. The hat doesn't do anything. What — you think it's a *magic* hat or something?'

'I'm a man. I know how to drive,' Eric said with dignity from beneath the floppy brim of the hat.

'Perhaps he does know how to drive,' said Penny, as though he wasn't with them.

'Yes,' agreed Eric. 'I do. But I'm not supposed to.'

'All right — when? When did you last drive a car?' Nick asked peremptorily.

'I can't remember. But I know how and I passed my test and everything. And I want to get home too. I'll give it a go. I don't want to but I will.' He tried to reassure them. 'It comes back to you. Like falling off a bicycle.'

'What's that supposed to mean?'

'It's a saying. Are you going to let me drive?'

'It isn't a saying — you're all mixed up again!'

'Let him have a go, Nick. We let you have a go and I don't think he could do much worse.'

'He's been a complete waste of space and now you're going to let him wreck your mother's car!'

'I want to help,' said Eric. 'I'm feeling awful.'

'Yeah — well — you're looking pretty awful!' And Nick got the giggles, as Penny had earlier.

When they had rearranged themselves in the car with Nick sitting in the front passenger seat beside Eric, the new driver announced the method he would use to drive the car. Now the moment had come he was rigid with nerves and when he turned his head to Nick it was as if he had a crick in it.

'I'm going to let my mind go a complete blank.'

'Oh.' And Nick giggled again.

In the effort of wiping his mind clean, Eric's face

registered a wide range of emotions. His expressions were so arbitrary and alarming that Nick began to feel the disguising hat was a good idea after all.

When there came a space in the traffic and they pulled out, Penny could have shut her eyes and imagined it was still her brother at the wheel. Since her eyes were open, she could see the difference between the two drivers: Eric's objective was to stay smack in the middle of the road.

'Keep me informed, Penny,' he said through clenched teeth. She was enough in tune with him to understand that he was thinking of her function as navigator.

Nick was vocally critical of Eric's driving skills or lack of them. It was not a hindrance, as, unlike Nick, Eric was grateful for all the help he could get and did not mind being kept posted of the dangers presented by the traffic, or being prompted what to do at any given time.

Further than that, it became clear that without such contributions the journey would be cut short by an accident of one kind or another: Eric had no especial fear of right turns since he did not weigh up his chances when making them, relying wholly on his passengers to tell him when it was safe to go and then going with a will. Whenever it became necessary to halt, he practised a vigorous emergency stop, so that to confine fellow motorists to an acceptable level of abuse Penny and Nick had to learn the precise moment at which to give the command.

The sensation of being a team in charge of the car was exhilarating after a while.

It was only when they were ensconced in the middle lane of the motorway, leaving London, that Eric made use of his rearview mirror. Penny herself had been looking into it from time to time, drawn to her image there as backseat passengers are at some stage on a long journey. Darkness was gathering and the lights of the oncoming vehicles swept across her face like beams from a lighthouse, showing the blue patches of fatigue under her eyes and a deepening bruise on her cheek, where the narrow man had pressed her into the glass of the funeral parlour. This was the image Eric sought out in the mirror. His eyes went straight to her every time and she would at once switch her gaze to the road ahead, uncomfortably conscious of his mournful stare; the stare that had eaten into her when they were in the underground train.

It was no longer a matter of life and death to act as Eric's driving advisors, yet after some mutual congratulations about extricating themselves from London, conversation was sparse.

'How's your hand, Nick?' Eric asked slowly, finding it hard to steer and talk at the same time.

'It's OK.'

The sliced area of flesh was becoming hot and in other circumstances would have been a worry to him. He had more pressing concerns, however.

'I suppose a little more speed's out of the question, Eric? If we want to get there in time. I don't want those guys to get to Dad before we do. If he's there. . .'

'You. . .want me. . .to go faster?' Eric asked.

'Yeah.'

'All right, Nick.'

CHAPTER 12

THE STRAIN of keeping up to a steady seventy miles an hour made a zombie of Eric. Every yard was torture to him, since in his own mind the car was driven not by its engine but by a supreme effort of his own will-power.

He fossilized into a human-shaped extension of the steering wheel.

As far as she knew, Penny was comparatively relaxed, but her grip on the bag of coins was almost as fierce as Eric's on the wheel.

By this time they were travelling along the A1 and it was as dark as midnight. Nick's eyes were on the dashboard and the green iridescent needle of the fuel gauge.

'We're going to have to stop.'

'Not *now*, Eric!' Penny said quickly, just in case. 'What is it, Nick?'

'Petrol.'

'Oh no! What are we going to do?'

'What do you think? Stop and get some.'

The next service station was as brightly lit as if it had been on fire. Nick insisted on wearing the hat again while he put in five pounds' worth of petrol.

It was left to Penny and Eric to make payment. An Asian in blue overalls served them in the mini-market attached to the garage.

'Hold the bag open, Eric. I'll count.'

The Asian grew impatient. 'I can't take coppers.'

'It's legal though, isn't it?' Penny said bravely.

'I can do what I like.'

'We've got the petrol already.' She was apologetic, forcing herself to smile at the man. 'Sorry.'

'Well... No pennies. How am I going to get rid of pennies?'

'We might have to give you some. Sorry.'

Nick got into the car, behind the wheel. Wearing the hat it seemed the place to be, and after the long break from driving he felt up to it again. He couldn't do any worse than Eric...

He looked over to the payment counter in the mini-market and saw Penny and Eric attempting to count out money while being jostled by drivers anxious to pay by credit card and get on their way.

While his attention was on the mini-market Vincent's estate car sped by on the fast lane of the highway.

Graham was walking about the house. It would not be true to say he was pacing, as fathers were once supposed to pace while they waited for a child to be born; he was too tired and had slowed to a shuffle. But he had to keep on the move.

He found himself in Penny's room again. He had searched the house for clues to the whereabouts of his children, as thoroughly as they had searched it for their Christmas presents, and with as little success. One of Penny's suitcases was open on the bed, where he had let it lie after going through it. He picked out a hairbrush and held it in his hands as though it was a delicate, animate object.

'Oh, my little girl,' he murmured.

He wore a sombre expression as he pondered again her absence. She would be with Nick, wherever she was. Perhaps they'd gone to a film: that was the most cheerful option he could come up with, though his mind tended towards more negative imaginings. It came to him that the hairbrush, in the way he was holding it, looked very much like a hedgehog.

'My little girl,' he murmured again.

It was no use. He couldn't feel a thing for her.

He threw down the brush into the suitcase and wandered into the corridor. He couldn't expect to feel so very much for Penny, could he? He hardly knew her. That must be the reason. With Nick, it was different, of course.

He went into his son's room, preparing himself to feel some strong emotion, but he was thinking, 'I've left on every light in the house. How wasteful...And which of them broke the kitchen phone? Do they think I'm made of money?'

Nick's room was appallingly untidy. Forgetting that he himself had been the cause of some of the mess, made in the course of his search, Graham got angry with Nick. To be so careless when you lived with your father, who had to trust you to do as much as you could for yourself...it wasn't fair.

But why wasn't he feeling any emotion other than savage irritation? He never knew how he was going to feel these days, but it was always much too much or much too little. Perhaps in this instance he was being protected by a defence mechanism — he didn't want to give way to the darker possibilities posed by the truancy of the children. But they weren't children any more... Probably it wasn't even *required* that he worry about them. He didn't know...he no longer knew how you were meant to react to things.

He set to work to tidy the room and the activity buried still deeper whatever it was he was really feeling.

Driving was easy when you were in a steady stream of vehicles all going in the same direction. It was strange how your mind could take little excursions from the matter in hand, though... Just now Nick was thinking about Penny. Penny and the pennies... She had had to use all her powers of persuasion to get the man in the service station to accept the loose change. Poor Penny. Actually, she wasn't a bad sister to have, if you had to have one at all. Actually...she was OK.

He said, 'I still don't understand why you had to have
the hat when you were driving, Eric. No one's going to
think you're too young to drive.'

'It wasn't that. People might see how I was feeling.'

' "Dreadful"?' Nick was quite lightheaded. Lack of
food, it would be.

'Scared, Nick. I'll be glad to get back home, I can tell
you. Back to all my things...'

'What things? You haven't got any things.'

Eric was hurt. 'I've got a radio. And a television. Things
to sit on... A cooker.'

'Self-igniting,' Nick remembered.

'Yes. I've got more things than I know what to do with.
I've got table lights... And tables... and—'

'Yeah. All right, Eric.'

As he did every now and then, Eric picked up on a
phrase. He twisted his body to look at Penny in the
obscurity of the back seat. 'Are you all right, Penny?'

'Yes. Very tired.'

'You'll be glad to get home too. There's no place like
home.'

They had reached Baldock and the lorry driver's haven,
Jack Hill's Café, with its huge car-park and shanty town
appearance.

In the café itself Vincent watched Colin roll himself a
cigarette.

'Get a move on.'

'What's the hurry?' Colin was feeling a trifle sick, but
benign. Vincent had tracked him down in a South London
pub where he had been all day.

Vincent saw him drop shreds of tobacco on to his
trousers. Some status symbol. But he would not break the
rule about smoking in his vehicle, not for a member of
the Royal family, let alone this dull lump of humanity, so
here they were.

His acute sense of hearing drew in a low conversation between two men at the next table.

'One doz. You agreed.'

'I didn't come all this way for less than a gross.'

'It's on the computer, Des. I can't risk it.'

'What's the difference? Either way you're short.'

'No can do. They've been laying drivers off at the depot.'

'We used to do a whole rail.'

'Not any more.'

'I got to have more than twelve.'

A little transport scam. Arrive at the outlet with a short order. Garment trade, this one was. After a while they'd go out to one of the lorries in the car-park and the man with the money would open up the boot of his car. Vincent would have liked to know how the men resolved their difference, but he was burning to get on. It wasn't that he needed Colin with him — he could handle Graham all right on his own — but he wanted the extra man so that Graham was in no doubt his number was going to be called and there was nothing he could do about it. Psychological advantage...or, to put it another way, outnumber the little nerd. Or, put it another way, make him suffer.

'What's so funny?' Colin asked.

'Nothing.'

'So — what we going to do when we get there? You're not going to cut him, are you? I don't fancy that.'

'It's not your worry. Just stand by to bundle.'

'You should've forgotten about it. Wiped it off.'

'No. Look — he'll have things there, won't he? Well, we're the bailiffs — take what we want.'

'What — you mean goods to the value of?'

'I mean what we want.'

'Yeah... Well — he can't argue much can he?'

Vincent smiled again. 'It don't matter if he does.'

'Not so fast, Nick — please.'

After passing through Royston Nick had gained the confidence of one who is in familiar territory, and when they turned off the main road into the narrower byways that led home, he became positively reckless. Speeding along a narrow lane at this moment, they were swallowed in the onrush of an avenue of trees. It was like travelling down the luminous green throat of some monstrous sea serpent. The trees appeared to accelerate towards the car as they were sucked into the diffused cocoon of light cast by the headlamps.

'Please. I mean it, Nick.'

'I know these roads like the back of my hand.'

'We don't even know he's there. *Please.*'

Nick ignored her. All at once a hare started out from the trees and sprang on to the road. Nick braked and for a second the hare's startled eyes were turned to wet rubies by the headlights. The animal pelted down the road in front of the car, feinting left and right with no intention of leaving the straight and narrow.

They were about to hit the hare when Nick pumped the brakes again and they slewed into the verge. The car sprang about like the hare in front of them and it was chance that bounced them back on to the road, where they skidded to a halt.

The hare jumped back into the trees.

Eric rubbed his head. During their fairground excursion on the verge, all three of them had smacked their skulls into the roof of the car.

'You were going too fast, Nick.'

'Of course he was!' Penny's voice quivered with shock and righteousness.

'Sorry, everyone.' But Nick was exhilarated rather than contrite.

When they started off again some part of the car scraped on the road and the engine sounded like that of a sports car.

'I think the exhaust's fallen off,' Nick said, more subdued.

174

'Thanks a lot, Nick! What's Mummy going to say?'

'I think we could worry about that later. We're nearly there now, anyway.'

'Where's the village?'

'We don't go through it the way I'm going.'

They came to the end of the tree-lined road and turned into a lane which was still narrower. It was a straight pencil line drawn between sugar-beet fields of Brobdingnagian proportions. The beet had recently been harvested and the earth was naked. Penny shivered. The scale and the emptiness of the dark, level landscape made it seem instantly colder.

After twenty minutes Nick said, 'Winter wheat. We're there.'

'What do you mean?' said Penny. The grinding of the car on the road had been a soporific, beating her into passivity.

'He's right, Penny—that's the crop they're growing round us,' Eric said. He sounded nervous. 'They're growing winter wheat this year.'

'Look!' Nick said. 'That light! That's the house! It's on fire, or something!'

Instinctively he put his foot down hard on the accelerator and the car grated along faster. There was a distinct glow on the horizon, Penny saw.

'I think flames would move about a bit more,' Eric said after a while. 'Actually, I think your dad's home...'

From the sound of it, Graham was a more fearsome proposition than a fire.

There were no more turns for Nick to make, left or right. The road wound round to the cottage in a gentle arc; and within a short space of time the blaze of light was reinterpreted as a house in which every curtain was open and every light was on. The nearer they got, the stranger it looked; exposed and characterless, a shell.

For Nick, it was not like coming home at all. He felt a swirl of nerves in his stomach. Perhaps the cottage looked

175

like this because those men were carrying out one of their thorough searches. The car seemed louder than ever.

'I'm going to stop here.'

'Good idea,' Penny said. 'We wouldn't want him to see Mummy's car like this.'

'Yes. Good idea,' said Eric, for other reasons.

Nick steered on to the heavy grass of the verge. There was an increase in the scraping under the chassis of the car. He hauled on the wheel and managed to park so that only the most careless driver could side-swipe the damaged vehicle.

A keen wind nipped at their ankles as they got out. 'Um... Just take a little look, I think,' Nick said.

'Good idea,' said Eric.

Penny squeezed out from behind the driver's seat. The carrier bag of coppers dropped heavily and jammed the seat mechanism, so that she couldn't push it back.

'I can't...'

'Leave it,' said Nick.

In front of the house the hedgerow was kept trimmed — by Eric — to the height of a low fence. Penny was surprised to see that both her brother and the gardener stooped low as they came to this point.

'What...?'

'Shut up, Penny. Just having a look.' Nick spoke quietly.

For how long, Penny wondered. The cold began to cramp the muscles used to maintain their stooped posture while they peered over the hedgerow into the bright spaces of Graham's sitting-room.

'There,' breathed Nick.

His father had appeared in the doorway from the hall. He was talking, so surely someone was with him. Even at this distance he did not look his normal dapper self. He did not come any further into the room. Something about the small movements he made with his head indicated that he was talking to himself.

It was unpleasant, spying on him in this way and Penny

said, 'Can't we go in now? He's worrying about us — you can see.'

'Yuh. It's OK, I guess,' Nick said. He and Penny straightened up, just as Graham turned and walked back into the hall.

Unable to view the goings on in the house, Eric remained crouched below the level of the hedgerow. 'Well, um, Nick...old chap,' he whispered heartily. 'I think — if you don't mind — I'll be getting along now...if you don't mind.'

Nick looked down at him blankly. 'Why?'

'Oh...well...I don't think he's going to be very pleased with me, you see. Going along with you like that. So — well — I'm really looking forward to going home. That's all right, isn't it? I can walk it in no time — you don't have to worry about me.'

'Well, if you say so...'

Eric nodded, still bent over.

'Yes. It'd be best.'

'Thank you for coming,' Penny said.

'Yeah — thanks, Eric. I really appreciate it.'

'That's all right. It was...' Words failed him. 'Bye-bye.'

They watched him trot off like a big, shy nocturnal animal: a badger, perhaps. He kept low to the ground long after the hedgerow regained its usual height.

It might have been the spectacle he provided, or it might have been a feeling that he deserved more than this furtive exit after what they had been through together, but they watched until he was lost in the darkness.

Then Nick said, 'To be honest, Penny, I'm not sorry to see the last of him. You feel so responsible for him.'

Penny did not answer this, although she too was relieved they would not be encumbered with Eric when they faced their father. She said, 'Shall we go in, then?'

'Better had.'

'What are we going to say?'

'To Dad? Explaining things? You should be asking, how is he going to explain things to us.'

177

The irresistible temptation to walk quietly up the path was at odds with Nick's air of resolution.

At the door they each waited for the other to take action.

'Do we ring the bell, or what?' Penny whispered.

'Sure,' Nick said, nearly as quietly.

He pressed the bell firmly and for a long time. Graham's footsteps to the door were frighteningly fast when they heared them. He threw open the door, gave a small involuntary whimper and slapped Nick hard across the side of the head. 'Get in! Get in here!'

He grabbed the leather jacket and hauled Nick over the threshold. Then he pushed him down the hall, cuffing at his ear between shoves.

'You're a disgrace! What do you think you're up to! How dare you! How *dare* you!'

Penny was ignored. She would not abandon Nick and there was, in any case, nowhere to go; so she followed them into the kitchen. Graham had been pushing Nick towards the sitting-room, but Nick had taken another direction in trying to get away from the hitting.

She arrived in the room in time to see Graham give his son one last, trembling cuff on the head.

'I don't know what to say to you. You...you've betrayed me. You've let me down!'

The words weren't enough and he flexed his hand again.

Nick yelled, 'I've betrayed *you*? I've let *you* down? You're a fake and a phoney and a liar — that's what you are!'

'That sort of talk's not going to get you anywhere. Where have you been? What have you been up to?'

Nick looked for a path into the conversation he wanted to have. 'Why did you sell the car?'

'You tell me where you've been, or —'

'I'll tell you why you sold it. Because you've got no money. You've been sacked from your job and we're broke!'

'Now wait a minute. That's not true. Who have you been talking to?'

'Mr Sheridan. You stole from him.'

'*What?*'

'You stole money from the company.'

'That's filth. You don't believe that. Do you know what kind of man Sheridan is? What he did to me?'

'I know what kind of man you are!'

'What's that supposed to mean?'

'We know everything about you. Me and Penny. We found out.'

Graham turned, following Nick's gaze.

'You. You little swine. You did this—you put him up to it. Anything to make him feel bad about me.'

He came close to Penny, bearing down on her with a stare of hatred.

'You're your mother's child. She doesn't like me.'

She flinched a little. He smelt unwashed and his eyes didn't seem quite to focus on her own. He looked away. 'What on earth does it matter what you think. *I* know the truth of it. That's what matters.' He went to the kitchen table and leant on it as if he was too tired to stand unsupported. 'Go to your rooms. Both of you. We'll talk about. . .about it all later. Just get out of here.'

Nick's voice was steady again. 'No. We'll talk now.'

Graham propelled himself away from the table. 'You'll do as I say!'

'Why?'

'I'm your father and you owe me respect.'

'And what do you owe us?'

'Don't twist it around. You've let me down. Let's get it quite straight who's the injured party here—me. I trusted you implicitly, and you have betrayed that trust. On the whole I think I'm being very good about it.'

'Yes. You trusted me, and I trusted you.'

'Yes! Well. . .no longer!'

'You're hooked on gambling, aren't you, Dad.'

Graham became frantic. 'Who told you that? Who? Where did you go? Who have you been talking to?'

'Everyone.'

179

'Where?'

'We went to London.'

Penny said, 'We saw your flat.'

'We know you've gambled away all your money.'

'Now that simply isn't true!'

'We looked through your papers,' Penny said. 'That's why we went to London.'

'Oh, I see — yes! To spy and. . .I don't know who you've been talking to but I can tell you that the only person who knows what he's talking about is me.'

'Dad,' Nick said, 'we didn't go to London to spy on you. We went there to find you. You didn't come home. It was Christmas, Dad.'

Graham's eyes flickered all over the room and his jaw went slack. With a prodigious effort of will-power he composed himself.

'I don't understand what you're talking about — this gambling idea. . .Nick — I'm sorry if I went off at the deep end, but you must understand how worrying it is for a parent when his child — his children — go off as you did. Now, about the gambling. All right — I lost my job. That's true enough. But you can appreciate how embarrassing that was — how I couldn't bring myself to tell you. Anyway, there I was, redundant through no fault of my own and I had to find a way to make money.'

Graham looked earnest, inviting sympathy. 'It seemed to me that my skills could be used in a survey of gambling — some articles like your mother writes. Obviously I came across some pretty strange people and quite obviously you've talked to some of them. I'm your dad, Nick, and I love you and you have to believe that these people can be vicious. Spiteful. Whatever it is you've heard it's only gossip from ignorant and envious people — people who resent me for one reason or another. Just believe me, Nick. That's what friends are for — and we're friends, aren't we?'

He looked so much like his old self that Nick wavered.

Penny said, 'But you did gamble. You like gambling.'

Graham shot her a glance of brilliant malevolence and it was his ill fortune that Nick saw it.

'Yes...' said Nick. 'You did. You gambled a lot.'

'All right...all right...yes — I got interested — of course I did. But I applied science — I've made a whole study of it on the computer — really just for interest. As for actual gambling, I hardly do it at all.'

'You never wanted to write articles,' Penny said, more passionately than she had expected. 'That's lies — you must have been losing money for years!'

'Yes,' Nick said, charged up again. 'If you hardly do it at all, how come you lost all your money?'

'You don't know that! I didn't...I haven't!'

'You have! We saw your bank statements — we saw everything!'

Graham resorted to screaming anger. 'I've given you everything you ever wanted! I've sacrificed my life for you! If it hadn't been for you I'd still have a job — I spent too much time on you — if I'd been free of you there's no knowing how far I might have got! You're ungrateful and —'

'You liar...liar!' Nick screamed back.

In the study Vincent quietly unplugged the phone. He had no way of knowing that it was not functioning. The front door had been open so they had walked in. They had experienced trouble in finding the house, but now they were here everything was going very nicely.

'Nice computer,' Colin remarked.

'Yeah.'

'Better shut the curtains, hadn't we?'

'Yeah, may as well.'

CHAPTER 13

THE CHROME surfaces of the kitchen bounced glaring light around the room; a space filled with the sounds of voices raised high in passion. Beyond this space the bare windows showed the sky to be made of black steel.

'You said,' Nick was shouting, 'you said I had to put up with you being away a lot because you were fighting for promotion and that would make our life better! That's what you said!'

'I can't talk to you if you won't listen to reason!' his father yelled back, unreasonably. 'Everything I ever did was for you!'

'Including all the lies? Like that one?'

'Stop calling me a liar!'

'You're sick, Dad! That's what that Paula woman said!'

This made Graham wilder than ever. Once again he raised his hand. 'Come here! Come here!'

'Please!' said Penny helplessly. 'Please.'

Graham was trying to get at Nick, with the kitchen table between them. Nick stepped back and Graham came around the table, brushing Penny aside. He chased Nick around the table until they were back where they started.

'Don't you hit me again! I'm not a kid!'

'I'll do what I like!' Graham shrieked and made his hand into a fist.

'If anyone's going to do any hitting around here it'll be me,' said Vincent.

Long and narrow, he stood in the doorway to the hall. Right by the side of his head was Colin's blurred and sweaty face, seeming to sit on Vincent's shoulder like a ball of meat.

Silence filled the room like an invisible gas.

Vincent stepped forward. 'What's first, Col?' he enquired lightly.

Colin came to stand beside him. 'Phone's bust already in here,' he observed.

The Hodges were locked to the spot as he went to the kitchen dresser and opened one drawer and then another. It was a small procedure of his to check where knives and other potential weapons were kept. Not that he expected a serious scuffle in this house, with this kind of people. He threw a handful of knives into the far corner of the room. By chance one of them stuck, quivering, in the skirting board.

Vincent said, acting very gentle, 'Did you really think you were going to get away with it?'

Graham stared at him, transfixed as the hare had been on the road.

'Nobody welshes on me. Not a soul, Graham old chap.'

The last sentence was delivered in a bad imitation of a public school accent.

Graham looked at Nick and Penny and said pathetically, '*Now* will go to your rooms?'

Vincent smiled. 'No. We're all staying here. Until you give me two thousand pounds.'

'It isn't two thousand pounds.' Graham instantly became more assertive, the aggrieved middle-class householder who has been overcharged.

'Near enough. I'm going to call it two thousand pounds.'

'I'll write you a cheque just to get rid of you. I just want you out of here.'

'Cheque's no good, Graham, old chap. You got no money.'

'If you knew that, why did you come here?'

'Oh, we'll get to that, don't worry.'

Penny said, 'I'm sorry, Daddy. It's my fault they're here.'

'What?'

'We got her diary. With your address.' Vincent looked at Penny. 'You don't want to be hard on yourself. I'd've got him — somewhere. With a habit like he's got, you can't keep yourself out of sight for long.' He looked around the room. 'I want something against this door, Col.' He indicated the hall door, which had no lock.

Colin took stock of the room. 'It's all tied down, Vinny.'

'Use the fridge.'

For no good reason it seemed safest to do absolutely nothing. The three Hodges thought hard but stayed where they happened to be standing. Vincent seemed so confident — so competent — that they let him take charge.

They watched Colin heave at the tall white box. The door swung open and two eggs fell out and broke on the floor as he began to haul the fridge to the hall door. He rocked it from one angle to another to frogmarch it to its destination and more items of food and drink cascaded to the ground. The electric lead tore itself free from the plug, which remained pinned into its socket on the skirting. Only when the heavy white box had been jammed against the door did Vincent go to the back door to lock and bolt it, while Colin took his turn to monitor the Hodges.

In the silence they heard Vincent humming a plaintive melody. Graham recognized it as the song 'Vincent' and stray lines from it came back to him, unbidden. 'Starry, starry nights. . .And when no hope was left in sight. . . This world was never meant for one as beautiful as you. . .'

Vincent stopped humming. 'Now then. Go and stand near the girl, Col.'

'You keep away from her,' said Nick and he got to her first.

'I don't want to hurt you, sonny,' Colin said.

'Don't make them angry, Nick,' said Graham. 'They won't do anything if you don't antagonize them.'

'Yes, Vinny?' Colin queried.

'Get him away.'

Colin put his hand on Nick's chest. Nick tried to strike it away and found himself flying backwards across the room. He knocked into a chair and fell over. His legs tangled themselves in those of the chair and by the time he was on his feet again Colin was behind Penny, with a firm hold on her arms. Nick started towards him again, warily.

'Don't do it, son,' said Vincent. 'She might get hurt if my friend has to look after you too. He's only got one pair of hands... Pick up the chair, sit on it, or she'll get hurt. Bound to.'

Nick said, 'Sorry, Pen,' and did as he was told.

'Leave my children alone!' Graham shouted. 'You've got no quarrel with them!'

Vincent walked to him and got up close, as he liked to. 'That's true enough. "Don't make them angry", you say. Well, it's a bit late for you, isn't it? You already made me angry. Now, I'll tell you what I'm going to do. I've done a little costing, and I figure I can pack away about a grand's worth of your stuff into my car. That's the telly, the computer — that's quite nice, that is — sound system...'

Graham blurted. 'That's just stealing!'

'It's worth more than a K, as it happens,' Vincent continued, 'but the question is what I can get for it. So, call it a grand. Well, that leaves us only halfway there, doesn't it?' He answered his own question, 'Yes, it does, old chap. And that leaves me very unsatisfied.' He reached carefully into his pocket. 'So I'm going to cut you.'

A lawnmower crashed through the kitchen window, bounced off the stainless steel sink and dropped heavily to the floor. Eric followed the old hand-mower in, vaulting the wall as though the window did not exist; which it did not now, much. He too bounced off the sink and landed on the floor. Unlike the mower, he did not come to rest. He came straight for Colin.

Used as he was to physical conflict, there was something about Eric which gave Colin pause. Penny felt herself twisted round until she formed a human shield between the two men. Eric shot out the palm of his hand straight

185

past her head, and Colin and she collapsed in a heap. Colin was moaning.

Eric's face was marked by a long red line oozing blood, where the jagged window had cut him. He had been making unintelligible growling sounds like a guard dog teased beyond endurance; now he bellowed, 'You do not hurt a kiddie!'

Vincent stared at him, appalled. There was something chillingly proficient in the way he was advancing, with his leading shoulder held low and his head tucked behind it. His other hand, the right, was cupped at his chest as if he was hiding a playing card from Vincent. It seemed impossible that this animal of destruction was the meek, tramp-like figure of their encounter in Graham's flat. Eric's dark eyes did not so much as blink when Graham seized the chance to duck away from the confrontation.

Vincent engaged the blade of his artist's razor-sharp cutter. At this moment it seemed to be about as fearsome as a water pistol.

Eric's advance slowed until he was barely moving. Behind him, Nick had gone to the drawers Colin had examined and had pulled out a skewer. He held it out. 'Eric! Here!' Eric did not look round.

The centre of Colin's face was a mess, but in the midst of his pain he had taken a firm hold on Penny's leg, so that she could not get to her feet. Graham went to try and pull her free and Nick dropped the skewer and joined him.

Feeling nauseous, Nick trod on Colin's wrist and he let go with a whimper. They pulled Penny back to the dresser.

'All right! That's enough!' Graham yelled.

'You won't stop him now,' said Nick softly. 'He's in the army again.'

They watched the two men in the centre of the room. Vincent took a small step in, holding the little blade at shoulder height and it appeared that Eric would back away. Then he took a rapid step forward on his right foot and as Vincent darted in, transferred the weight to his left and pivoted in a fast circle with his right leg sweeping round like an axe to chop behind Vincent's knee.

Vincent went down like a dynamited factory chimney.

'You'll never hurt kiddies again!' Eric roared and he picked up the mowing machine as if it was made of polystyrene and raised it high above his head.

'No! Eric!'

By some alchemy Nick's voice held true authority and Eric became motionless, the iron weapon still held high. Keeping the same position, he turned to look at Graham, with an expression of agony on his face.

'Look what you've made me do!' Tears filled his eyes. 'I hate you!'

And he cast the mower across the room, ridding himself of it as if it was radioactive. While it was still in the air he was bending down to plunge his fingers into Vincent's suit. The mower landed with a crash and Vincent took its place in the air, lifted up as though he was a baby. Eric shook him and spoke to him in a voice still gutteral with emotion.

'Get in your car and go. If I want to I can put my hand into you and pull out your backbone. I know how to do that. And I'm a gardener,' he added, 'so I can bury you after and no one will find you because I know where to dig. I'll bury you both.'

He tossed Vincent in the direction of the mower and Vincent landed on it painfully. 'Colin!' he called. 'Col!'

With the speed of a gigantic gerbil, Eric scurried to where Colin was getting to his knees. With rather more effort than with Vincent, he picked up the status symbol and hurled him clumsily at his mentor. There was a comic strip element in the way the two visitors lay in a heap with the mower, but real violence was ugly and unfunny, Nick saw.

Eric satisfied himself that the two men were unlikely to attempt rapid action. He turned and came slowly towards

Graham, Nick and Penny. His eyes had lost their fire. He said to Graham, 'I'm afraid I won't be doing your gardening any more.'

'Ah,' Graham said faintly.

'Why did you come back, Eric?' Nick asked.

'The car passed me on the road. I saw it was them. Or. . .I knew it was them. Then I had to hurry. I saw him locking you in, so. . .'

'Thanks, Eric.'

'I feel dreadful. I feel very uncomfortable with myself.' He passed a hand across his forehead and smeared blood over his face without noticing it. 'Got to. . . Could you open the door now?'

'Well, I think the thin one's got the key.'

'Oh.' Eric went and lifted Colin again, Colin tried to hit him and he did something to Colin's arm.

The way was clear to stand Vincent up against the wall. Eric took hold of the man's face quite gently and said in a pleading way, 'Please remember what I told you. Now you will, won't you?'

He kept his hand on Vincent's face while he went through the pockets of the suit. Finding it, he tossed the back door key to Nick. 'Open up. Now, you two. Come along. You're going to walk out of here now.'

It was not, in fact, that simple for Vincent and Colin. Vincent limped very badly and had evidently hurt his back on the mower and Colin was finding it difficult to breathe. He held his injured arm gingerly against his side.

Nick went back to Graham and Penny after he had opened the door. Vincent turned back with a look of hatred for Graham. He wanted to say something to impress, couldn't think of anything and was shoved out of the house by Eric.

Eric turned back too. 'Got to stay with them. I'll watch the house for you tonight. You won't see me, but I'll be here. But you won't see me. Goodbye, Penny. It was nice to meet you.' His face crumpled itself up with some strong emotion. 'It's dreadful. I wish...' Eric shut the door behind him and they would never know what it was he wished.

It was utterly quiet for several seconds.

'He didn't move the fridge,' Graham said stupidly.

'I think he thought he'd done enough,' Penny said.

No more words were spoken for a while. They felt empty after the violence and moved at an underwater pace in a slow, silent world.

Nick turned off the glaring overhead light. He moved the mower into a corner. Penny took a J-cloth and wiped at the food on the floor. Graham spent the time in washing his hands at the sink. He used quantities of washing-up liquid in the operation.

'Shall we get the fridge back?' Nick asked eventually.

Graham did not want to turn round. He squeezed out more detergent and washed his hands again.

'Pen?'

'Yes.'

Nick and Penny struggled with the big white box. They could barely move it.

'Please help, Daddy,' Penny said. She discovered she did not want to call him 'Daddy' any more — never again. Yet how else could she address him?

It did not matter much, since from his lack of reaction she might not have spoken at all.

'Dad! Come on!' Nick said urgently. 'Do you want us to be stuck in here forever?'

'Please help us,' said Penny.

He kept his back to them. 'Help you? You didn't exactly help me, did you? It's all your fault those men came here. You and your diary.'

'Well, it's not *all* my fault,' Penny said awkwardly.

Sudden passion overwhelmed Nick. 'Her fault? Her fault? You're lucky she's even speaking to you! They came here because of you — you and nobody else — because you've made a disaster out of your life. And mine. You're not good enough to clean her shoes, let alone blame her for the mess you put yourself in!'

They could not hear what their father said to that until he repeated it.

'I know.'

'What?' said Nick.

Graham was silent.

Nick walked over to him. When he was by Graham's side he looked back at Penny and she went to them.

Tears were flooding down Graham's cheeks. He would not remove his gaze from the tap, which was pouring water into the sink. 'I'm in bits. . .I've had it. I'm so tired. . .I've had enough. I'm sorry.' He tried to say 'I'm sorry' again but his emotion choked the words into a rising squeak and he surrendered to his feelings.

His tears went on and on.

It did not seem appropriate to comfort an adult. Instead, Penny put her arm around her brother's waist. She held on to him tightly and Nick's hand came across to rest on her enfolding fingers.

CHAPTER 14

THE LOW heels on their mother's sensible shoes clacked down on the polished floor of the hospital corridor. She strode along with the authority of a ward sister, at the least. On the way here Barbara had lectured them, teaching them to think of the place as a hospital. 'A psychiatric clinic is as much of a hospital as any building is whose function is to treat the sick. Your father has an illness — he is not simply selfish and obsessed. He is there as a sick man.'

Her children, once again second-class citizens, trailed in her wake. It had been three crowded weeks since Nick had walked to the village at the dead of night and telephoned their grandmother, setting in motion a train of events that had gradually dragged them back into a reality they were used to.

Nick's hand was in a fresh bandage. The cut made by the tomato can had turned septic and the resulting puff-ball of flesh had been lanced. It had been quite a drama. Penny was sure the bandage was no longer necessary. Trust Nick to find a way to first get, and then hold on to, the attention.

One evening she had been on her way to the kitchen for a late-night hot drink and she had overheard her mother and Tony in the front room. Barbara was saying, 'The hand's going to be OK, but, of course, Nick has some inner scars that may never heal. That's more worrying really, because he doesn't communicate to us about those.'

So what about her — Penny? Didn't she have inner scars too? Or wasn't she allowed them, because she had been for so long her mother's companion and was thus invisibly protected by the never-ending flow of wisdom and

191

understanding? Now, added to her mother's informed compassion, she had the Toy Boy to deal with and *his* brand of caring... But he wasn't the Toy Boy any more. He was Tony ('Call me Tony and we'll see how we go') and underneath the showiness of his interest and concern there was real interest and concern, Penny now knew. If he said some jargon like 'we all need our own space', he meant it and acted according to his pronouncements. He wasn't a father — but he didn't try to be: he tried to be a friend. Really they had been very lucky there. So far it was like having a lodger...in a way... Except that her mother was Barbara Marshall now, not Barbara Hodge any more and one day — a day Penny dreaded — she felt sure Tony would suggest (in a caring way) that they call him 'Dad'.

They went into a small room with glass windows looking back into the corridor and sat down on moulded plastic seats which had been sculpted to fit a human backside. An average backside, Penny wondered — or had someone modelled?

She was bored. Expecting to be nervous, she only wanted to get this done with. What was the point of dragging all the way out here to this converted country house, to look at their father as if he was an exhibit in a zoo.

On the journey, Nick had been quite impressed with their new car. On her swift return from the honeymoon their mother had been very good about that part of their trials, as she had been about all the rest.

'You should have told me. It didn't matter where I was or what I was doing. But I believe you did what you thought right at the time. You did your best and in a way I'm proud of you. I don't say it was wise — but you did your best.'

The new car was only just second-hand and if Nick approved of it obviously it had some status value... Penny knew him so well now. What would he be thinking as he sat looking out of the window on to the park-like grounds?

Probably going over some information technology problem. Though Graham's house was up for sale they had managed to hang on to the computer by saying it was Nick's and not his father's and Nick already spent an inordinate amount of time hunched over the keyboard, in the bedroom in Barbara's house that had once been a junk room.

Nick looked out at the grounds. What could it be like, stuck in this place. It was so quiet and peaceful here. Inside and out, the atmosphere reflected the virtues of tranquillity and contemplation. The building itself held a hush like some bookless library. His father had admitted himself voluntarily, but probably he would be restless by now. If he hadn't altered out of all recognition, he would be. He had so much energy...you had to admire that, if nothing else... It was hard to know what to think about Dad. What a mess he'd made. And how completely he had fooled Nick. Betrayed him, when you came down to it. All that stuff about being a team... He wasn't ill, he was just a selfish liar.

'I'm going to the loo,' Penny said.

'All right, darling. There's a ladies if you go on to the end of the corridor. Don't be too long.' Barbara smiled at her and Penny twitched her mouth dutifully in response.

Walking back to the visitors' room, curiosity got the better of her. At intervals along the corridor there were doors. They had no signs on them and it was impossible not to wonder what went on behind them. Was this one, perhaps, where they kept the drugs they used to quieten the dangerous patients? It was, after all, a psychiatric institution. It seemed to Penny that it would be a horrid stigma to carry, having been—what was the term—an *inmate* of one of these places...

Two of the doors were windowed, with thick wire-reinforced glass. The first of these rooms was empty and seemed to be some kind of viewing theatre, with rows of chairs set in front of several television monitors and a cinema screen hanging down from the back wall.

193

In the second room some kind of group discussion was taking place. A semi-circle of chairs faced a bearded man in a jeans jacket. Unwittingly sexist, Penny was surprised to see that about a third of the adults were women. They all looked attentive. It somehow reminded her of a primary school class. The man with the beard was—what was it?—a counsellor, but he had the underpaid enthusiasm of a teacher as he talked to the group. One could imagine he was saying, 'Who remembers what the little dog did on page six?'

She looked for her father in the therapy session but could not see him. One of the men in the group caught her looking through the window and smiled at her quite normally. She moved hastily away.

In the waiting-room Barbara offered Nick a sugar-free mint and he refused it. She always carried them and he hated to be offered them: it made him feel like a child again and he wasn't. Not any more.

Penny came back in and sat down again.

'All right?' Barbara asked.

'Mmn.'

They waited for Graham.

When he came, it was in the company of another man, a skinny fifty-year-old with a cockney accent. 'Here we are! See you later, then.'

'See you.'

Graham spoke very quietly. Never a big man, he seemed to have shrunk. No one could have accused him of being larger than life. He wore a baggy jumper and looked vaguely artistic.

He smiled nervously at his children.

Barbara said, 'Who was he? One of the staff?'

His voice was still low and he talked very fast, a little breathless. 'No. Another client, like me. Been here for a month longer. Something like that. They, um, they don't completely trust me. Not yet. Someone did a bunk the other night. Funny, isn't it.'

He did not sound as if he thought it was funny.

'And how are you?' Barbara said forcefully.

'Oh. . .' He sat down in a chair under the window, away from his family. 'Well. . .' He looked at Nick. 'It's nice to see you.'

'Hi, Dad,' Nick said in a colourless voice.

'That's a great jumper, Pen.'

'Thanks. It's new. Tony. . .'

'Did he? That was nice of him.'

'But how *are* you?' Barbara asked.

'Getting there, since you ask.' There was a dim echo of the old asperity there. 'But it isn't easy. I didn't mind you suggesting this because. . .because I wanted. . .because I needed to say some things. I don't know quite where I'm at, but I can see that I was. . .' A look of pain expressed the struggle he was having with this. 'I wanted to say I'm sorry. Mostly to you, Nick.'

Nick did not know how to cope with this public apology. Graham looked away from him and said to the world in general, 'They say it's not my fault. What they say is, I've got to forgive myself. It seems pretty cock-eyed to me.'

Barbara said, 'They have a very high success record here.'

His eyes settled on hers briefly. 'Trust you to know the figures. They keep asking. "Do you *want* to get well?" But the one you hear most is, "How are you feeling?" They never stop asking that. "How are you feeling". . .'

'Well, how are you feeling?'

He began to breathe very fast and then he stood up. 'I've got to go. Sorry. Thought I could handle it. Sorry.'

He left the room quickly.

There was a pause. Barbara said, 'It's not fair to kick him when he's down, but I must say we did come a long way to see him.'

They had come a long way and it seemed silly to march straight out again. It took some moments before a mutual resolve brought them to their feet. Barbara was about to say something when the bearded counsellor Penny had

195

seen came into the room. 'Hello, Mrs Marshall. I, er, I ran into Graham.'

'Running away from us, yes,' Barbara said.

'I've got a moment, if you want to talk.'

Barbara sat down again. Penny and Nick followed her example.

The man asked, 'You don't mind the kids listening in?'

'No. I'm all for it.'

'Good. So am I. And, believe it or not, Graham doesn't mind either. We thought this might happen...'

Barbara was tense. 'It's normal, I suppose? That kind of reaction to us?'

He laughed easily. 'I don't think we'll get too far just now by talking about what constitutes normality. Graham acted in a way that made him feel more comfortable, that's all.'

'Yes. He ran away,' Barbara said curtly.

The man used a smile to deflect this. He said, 'It's Nick and Penny, isn't it?'

They nodded. He looked at Barbara. 'What shall I do? Give them a run-down on what I've told you?'

Her opinion sought in this way, Barbara calmed down. 'That'd be good, yes.'

He looked back at Nick and Penny. 'I'm Derek. All right?' They nodded again.

'We think your father's going to be fine. But you have to appreciate just how big the problem is.' He went to the window and opened it. 'Not too cold for you?' he asked politely. 'Where shall I start...Well...we know quite a lot about guys like your dad. Like the fact that people with addictive tendencies tend to share common attributes and feelings. Among those is a very low self-worth. A very low opinion of themselves. And running alongside that is a phenomenal self-will. It's all rather contradictory, I'm afraid. What you will have seen in Dad is moments of enormous self-confidence alternating with the opposite — black despair. Would I be right?'

He was very encouraging.

'Yes,' Nick said.

'Well, what's weird is that we have to break through the self-will to get at the...at the emptiness he really feels inside. In other words, we have to destroy what confidence he has before we can help him, in a way. What this requires, initially, from Graham, is that he admits he can no longer manage his own life — he's got to own up that he's lost control. To do that means a kind of surrender. Well, he hasn't fully surrendered yet. He hasn't quite let go completely — if that makes sense. There's a part of him that still thinks that if he'd just had a bit more luck at crucial times everything would have been all right.'

Nick said tentatively, 'But...isn't that true?'

'No. He has a habit that's got beyond winning or losing. All he wants to do is gamble, as much as possible, as often as possible. That's what he's got to see. But, let me tell you, you two are very good news. What you achieved those weeks ago was a kind of — we call it a family intervention. You stepped in just as he hit rock-bottom and you confronted him with what was really going on. Without that breakthrough we wouldn't stand a chance. Other men and women with this problem can go down a lot further before they hit the truth about themselves — and of course some never do. So...I'm here to say thank you on your dad's behalf. And hopefully, one day he'll say it too.'

Barbara said suddenly, 'Would you believe me if I said that in the years we had together I never had an inkling of any gambling going on?'

Derek shrugged. 'Perhaps there wasn't. Perhaps he hadn't discovered it yet. Or perhaps he hid it from you. Just because he's an addict, it doesn't mean he's not very resourceful. They usually have to be.'

'It makes me feel foolish though.'

He was not interested in that. 'I'll tell you one other thing. It's a family illness. In one way or another, you will all of you have been affected. I think you should certainly consider the possibility of Nick, at least, joining a programme for children of compulsive gamblers.'

'But it's nothing to do with me!' Nick burst out. 'He's the one who's sick, or whatever it is — not me!'

The counsellor looked at him attentively. 'Well...see how you go.'

'Gratitude!' Nick said some months later.

'Sorry?'

'He was on about how amazingly grateful he is. He never stops.'

'Well, perhaps he is grateful.'

They were in Nick's room and Penny stood behind him where he sat at the computer, which was formatting floppy disks for future use. Nick had gone on from school for tea with his father and as usual had come back distressed.

'He doesn't have to go on about it all the time,' he said. 'Grateful for what, anyway? He hasn't got anything. No money, no job...what's he got to feel grateful about?'

'He feels better about himself.'

The computer stopped ticking and gave a shrill bleep of triumph. Nick removed one disk and inserted another. The formatting began again.

'He said he hoped he hadn't hurt me too much. He's so meek and mild. He used to be so positive. Now he wouldn't say boo to a goose. I hate the way he looks at me. So apologetic.'

'You have to accept him as he is now.' Penny tried out one of the terms Tony used: 'You mustn't be so judgemental.' It sounded about right in this context.

'It's all right for you. It's me he always wants to see.'

Penny could have said, 'Well, it's you he loves the most,' but it wouldn't have helped either of them. Graham was living in what was called 'a halfway house', where people found their feet in the world again after a period in a dependency clinic. Penny had only seen him once, for a cup of tea in a burger bar, and they had not had much to say to one another.

The computer ticked on in a perfect, dead rhythm. Nick had an aching, agitated feeling in his stomach. It was hard to believe that he had once been so proud of his father. The man was so pathetically tentative. In some odd way you would have almost preferred him to be how he was before.

'Hey,' Nick said suddenly, 'look.'

The last disk was formatted and he switched to the hard drive on the PC. Some rapid work on the keyboard brought him into the directory and file he wanted. 'Look at this. I finally managed to de-crypt it last night.'

All Penny saw were rows of figures. Nick went on, 'Know one of the things he was doing? He was looking for a golden number. That's the mathematician's equivalent of alchemy. Didn't get there of course, but it's fascinating, isn't it?'

All at once Penny felt unutterably depressed. 'If you say so. I'd better get on with my homework.'

In her own room she moved all the rubbish from the top of her desk and put it on the bed before she unpacked her school bag and laid out her French textbook and exercise book. She put a new ink cartridge in her fountain pen. That seemed to be enough for the time being — she had made a start... Nick was lucky; he zoomed through his homework. She knew he did so to show he had a low opinion of their school, but it was still impressive. You didn't have to worry for him when it came to keeping up with the work.

In other respects she did worry for him. He still hadn't made any friends. That didn't matter so much, because he and Penny were so close now. It was good to have a brother, a lot of the time. A companion your own age or thereabouts took the pressure off your relationship with your parents...parent. Remember that: parent. Tony was a friend and that was all.

199

Nick had been to a few groups set up for the children of gamblers and then given up on them. 'All that talk. Sounds like whining to me,' he said. That was another thing she half-admired about him. He had opinions and wasn't afraid to come out with them...except when he was depressed, which was quite often, and then he wouldn't communicate with anyone, not even her.

To her surprise, Barbara had not battled to make him stick with the group thing. It might be that pride made her think that she should be able to handle her children's problems herself. Intuition suggested that guilt played some part here. Maybe it wasn't too comfortable to dwell on the consequences of that wonderful honeymoon away from her children.

Penny's room faced out on to the little back garden, which looked at its best in the soft sunlight of an early summer evening. How lucky they were, she thought very consciously, that everything had turned out so well. The thought did not touch her emotions. She still felt low. Opinions...she wished she had some of her own. These days she was not sure about anything. The business of growing up seemed to be a learning process by which one knew less and less about more and more. Take those two ghastly men who had tried to hurt them. No one had been very interested. You'd have thought that the forces of justice would have wanted to get hold of them and — well — at the least, correct their attitudes. But no, they were allowed to go on behaving exactly as they wanted to, wherever they were...

Yes — she was anxious about Nick. It was a penalty of love, she guessed, to have worry as well. And yet...she was always anxious now. All the time... Not enough to talk to her mother, or Tony, but...just generally. She didn't seem to enjoy herself as she thought she had before. There was always this feeling that something might go wrong. She had a recurring nightmare she had not told anyone about. She was being pressed against the dark

200

window of the undertaker's shop and the tall narrow man was whispering to her. The most horrifying thing about the dream was that she could not hear what he was. saying.... It would be some black secret and she feared the night when she finally had to listen to it.

But they were lucky. Of course they were. Lucky! Think about Eric and how he had transformed into a kind of super-hero for them. Wasn't it frightening, how strong grown-up men were....

He had said they would not see him again that night and they hadn't; yet she, at least, had sensed his presence through those long hours. Since that time, every now and then she thought about him and a good feeling came over her. It was just nice to know he was in the world.

But reading between the lines, he was glad to be shot of them. Barbara had been to see him to say thank you and had come away cross. 'He just wanted me out of his house as soon as he could manage it without giving offence, as — no doubt — he would put it. Honestly, it amazes me that people like that aren't looked after. I think you were both very lucky. I remember seeing a programme...people with head injuries can be extremely unpredictable.'

Well, maybe... Though Penny had an idea that Eric had somehow latched on to some good things that others let escape them.... She remembered the way he ate, giving his full, satisfied concentration to every mouthful, and how he appeared to exist without questioning why he was or where he was, without any obvious needs, as undemanding as if he was an article of furniture or one of the plants he tended.

She remembered especially the joy that had suffused him when he recalled his golden times at the holiday camp. 'Fun at the pool...' You got a clear picture of simple pleasures, the way he had said it. She herself could not envisage taking such unalloyed pleasure in anything, ever again.

Nick seemed happy to let him have his own way; to let

him drop out of their lives. It hadn't seemed quite fair to Penny, although Nick did know him better than she did and would appreciate what he really wanted, she supposed.

She had decided they should write to him — just to thank him again, if no more than that. Nick had not been keen, but had given her the address. 'You write if you want to. Send him my regards if you do...'

So she had written. A long letter, with all their news. And she had sent him their love, because he deserved it. She had not really expected a reply and had given up on one by the time the very light envelope landed on the mat. He had written his name and address on the back of the envelope, as you do on an airmail letter.

Sitting here now, as the heavy red sun touched the skyline of roofs, Penny pulled open the bottom drawer of her desk and brought out the envelope. Actually, she should really get on with her homework...in a minute. Or maybe a minute or two.

She had let herself have a moment of expectation. There might be in this letter a little fragment of true wisdom one could hold on to, because for all his own anxieties Eric had this indefinable thing going for him. She had thought it was just possible that he would have written something that might make her feel...better.

Penny slipped the letter out of the envelope and unfolded it. The paper was lined and the writing was very big between the lines.

> Dear Penny,
> Thank you for your letter. I am glad
> you are well. I am very well too.
> It has been quite hot here but you
> can't have everything. It was nice
> of you to write.
> Yours faithfully,
> Eric Hope.

Well, so much for that. She put the letter back into the

envelope and put the envelope back in the drawer, taking care that it would not get bent.

Then she opened the French textbook and turned to page thirty.